T0064033

Bites for Muse, not a fast food

Bites for Muse, not a fast food

Short Stories

A M B A L E   N A G A

PARTRIDGE
A Penguin Random House Company

To order additional copies of this book, contact
Partridge India
000 800 10062 62
orders.india@partridgepublishing.com

www.partridgepublishing.com/india

Dedications.

(Captured reflection, post a recent wise advice by
a mourning NRI friend, to his next generation-
"To acknowledge and express affections at
apt times, before too late in life!")

'To mighty parents.'

In the mild spread of dim lights,
And percolating wine in dry throats,
Pure Sensitized moments sprang,
Amid seeping Sitar in gentle
stream. (1)

The culture nurtured in earnest,
Shaped some values in my subsist;
but,
The imbued legacy I inherited
largely,
Is the 'unalloyed love' induced
surely! (2)

In the solemn moments of
solitude muse,
With genuine tears flowing in
profuse,

A strange truth of foibles of humans,
Struck me like a bolt from
heavens. (3)

How I wish I had hugged you more,
Would have made you happy am
sure;
In lieu of the copious flow now,
Ought to have thanked often,
With 'a few pearls' in glisten. (4)

_____

Even when am free from the rare
spell,
I fondly ask: are not the parents
'mighty',
On par with the imaginary
'Almighty?'

_____

v

CONTENTS

AUTHOR'S FOREWORD

As an author, I have neither the audacity to be the ebullient sun radiating bright rays, nor the humility to be only a reflecting moon. Anyway, when the intents of the reader is on the contents, the author recedes like the drama director, behind the scenes. Surely, the ideas of great souls influenced and even overwhelmed in the life of the contemplative natured author.

Most of the stories covered are explored, but not fantasies. The creations are, 'possibilities', closer to real life. The choice and style are opted for the effective dealings, 'to illuminate the human facets' or '**with essence to ponder**' in the chosen topics; with a genuine motive for adding value to the readers.

The range of the domain includes music, philosophy, literature, painting, spirituality, social science, poetry, religion, history and astrology, apart from a few mundane zones. The **Style** preferred is 'Literary', with interwoven 'poems,' quotes' and 'powerful expressions', at selected places for effectiveness and emphasis, suiting native touch.

Importantly, I believe the readers are evolved and evolving always.

"The more evolved you are, the less you will agree or disagree with others, and the more you will gently sift through the fullness of what people are offering and take only what you need."   ---Bryant McGill.

Bangalore	Ambale Naga (Pen name).
June 2015	[Subbaramaiah Venkata Nagan.]

I thank my friends, Dr. Vidyasagar A. and Sri P.S. Nagaraja, for their valuables suggestions. My special thanks to Partridge and personnel associated, for their professional skills and personal touch, in my maiden venture.

Synopsis of stories

Locations: Places, in and around Bangalore and Mysore, India.

1. **Custodian**: An innate genius of 'words', Gowda, inspired by his English professors at the college and a brief stay at England, returns to become an authority as critic, with a self-assumed role of 'custodianship', to retain richness of the English language. By turn of events in personal life in the middle age, is in a quandary, either to roll back decades to rekindle his spontaneity and affinity to language of his soil or to sustain his present role, which has already won him exceptional accolades?

2. **Tippu Drop:** In the midnight at an infamous place, where criminals were pushed to perish and the hapless disillusioned end life by suicide, the aged Samaritan Arun is to decide his option, for the fate of a despicable person.

   "Judgement is deceit, a walk on razor edge, If heart melts it can be mercy, otherwise incisive intellect can make it brutal"?

3. **Bahadur:** In the poignant days of mourning of a captain in BSF, his father Bahadur, a Gurkha veteran himself, now with a civil establishment attached to defence ministry, bares a revelation on their traits. Gurkhas, otherwise known for their indomitable spirit in fights with spine chilling war cries, have a human face with an attitude -'Life is a simple dignity'.

4. **Maturity:** Satish, an objective middle aged prosperous intellectual, who has successfully learnt to tame stirring emotions to retain 'maturity', faces a litmus test in decades. Can he retain the courageous detachment in the imposing waves, when the loving daughter leaves for abroad after marriage, to settle?

5. **Beautiful people:** Nandu, aspirer of Doctorate in philosophy is forced to explore the human values of some 'beautiful people' encountered in his life. In the process realises that philosophy is not diluted or extinct, but shall survive as long as the human spirit prevails.

6. **Stinking Sandals.** Teenage Shambu in a memorable visit with his uncle, to uncle's mentor's funeral learns the glimpses of human selfishness, in its hollow nakedness.

7. **TM:** Rajath, a brilliant young alumni of IIT, working in design firm, gets fascinated by the experience of the seniors, and learns TM for symbiosis of 'relaxation' & 'concentration', and

personal empowerment. In light of analysis of his elder cousin, a psychologist' from US & with his 2 years' experience of practice, relooks into TM for a decision to continue or not?

8. **Musical moments**: The enigmatic gracious couple in end sixties with the poise of dancers, in their personal blissful musical moments in a party hall, induce soul searching moments in some onlookers of different ages. In the ambience of permeating music, with tunes to resonate in different moods, will they be able to unwrap trapped signals, modify misgivings, and discover new meanings in life?

9. **Dearest Delight:** With the conviction that in the chaotic life of exploded knowledge, to induce & sustain human values, and to make life bearable & meaningful, an introductory course is needed, Nandan, a philosophy professor makes a passionate lecture on his 'dearest delight'- philosophy. The engineering students in the final year are the audience with a choice to decide on enrolment?

10. **Guilt:** Raghu's download on YouTube, a fascinating truth of child's antics in womb, triggers recount on an episode in Grand ma's life, leading to the curious case of, which will prevail? Is it 'Nature's incline' or 'God's will'?

11. **Debate:** Ponnappa, a brilliant Dalit student of political science, soft hearted humanist, with a

legacy of people carrying human excretion and cleaning toilets for life times, dreams of changing social order by making religion irrelevant inspired by Plato's words – "Religion is a noble lie propagated by philosophic elite for ensuring social order". A classmate, who had felt his potential "to 'stir' the system, if not 'shake'," after two decades finds out the turbulent life of his friend.

12. **The Secret of the cellar:** Lalitha, a poor girl who is like a delicate and an adorable flower, "for lighting other candles of the house to glow in better houses" marries a wealthy businessman whose fancy is only her physical charm. In a few years, in a crisis of 'no comebacks', has to choose between her virtues or the legacy of the hidden secrets of the cellar, for her survival?

13. **The flower in the school:** Karthik, a young dreamer in a high school, in the tender age of undeveloped understanding and puzzling curiosity, in the proximity of a girl with champak flower, gets an awakening for his poetic gift. With the aroma surreptitiously following him into his college days, builds a beehive of poems, as sweet as honey, only to be shattered in a few years. Can his singing inner bird mute now and the sense of smell blocked, make a comeback?

14. **Purity:** Siddhi, a soul searching, truth seeking student of 'spritualty', in pursuit of the 5th step in 'Patanjali yoga', spends months on a hillock

and surroundings, on advice of his mentors. Near the small temple on the hillock, on a Sunday congregation of villagers, learns a facet of 'truth' from an innocent child of 8 years, which he couldn't fathom otherwise. Ends up in tantalising dilemma to continue his spiritual pursuit or not?

15. **Life of Artists:** A sensitive one inclined for arts, by chance becoming an IAS is in a fix to continue or to switch to art. But the wise ripened thespian inspires a deeper purpose in his professional life?

16. **Impractical:** Nagesh, an 'impractical', with a belief that notion of 'practical' is a deception to interpret for selfishness, is in a predicament after he returns from his Masters from USA, to join his loving wife?

17. **Painting:** Sheshu, a renowned artist, seeking an inspiration at Kerala for his best painting for the ensuing exhibition of his collections in a gallery, is in dilemma to choose between, the glittering idol of Lord Padmanaba, now famous for the $20 billion treasure or the legendary feminist of yesteryears 'Nangeli', who sheared her breast to die, protesting queer tax system on breast cover. Comes out with a stunning master piece depicting the horrifying truth of link between them?

18. **Religious:** The intellectual who adores for decades, the words, 'courage, serenity and wisdom', in an inspiring quote, suddenly, on an eventful day realises his limitation to fathom essence of them?

19. **Tutor:** The bright, ending prematurely his not so successful career, by exigency has to spend two years in his town. Learning the naked truth, 'equality in opportunity is a myth' for bright poor students, succeeds to tap the potential of some for two years. But sudden windfall and a feel of lack of appreciation for his services, puts him in a dilemma?

20. **Vedic school:** The 'Vedic school', in the vicinity of the culture city- Mysore, is the venue for exploring the fascinating facets of the ancient India's wisdom. John, an American student of gemmology, is exposed to some facets in the enormity of Vedas, including 'why humans', instead of 'what humans', along with his sphere of 'Jyothishy'. In the end, unexpectedly takes a humane decision to sustain the existence of the school, for its survival.

****

1. CUSTODIAN

The finals moments in the 'Spell Bee' competition, the Regional Finals gripped one and all. Most in the audience at the Chicago cultural hall are on the edge of their seats. The audience could view the triangularly seated Judge, the Pronouncer and the Speller, glancing one another, as the sequences proceeded.

More than the visual convenience, the fidelity in voice counts in the phonetics game. The 'diacritical 'marks of the dictionary needed to be adhered to, strictly. The pronouncer need to refrain, 'Archaic', 'Regional', and 'Stylistic' labels for the accents.

The game is a fascinating test for skills, passion and prolonged preparations.

Finally for the Indian audience and Indian viewers on the televisions, the win by a Bengali Boy, meant much more than the triumph. It is a pride for their identity in a place where 'innovation and competition' matters.

For the cluster of Indians, including Mukund, it is a high in jubilations, an emotional experience. They are all the acquaintances and the family of the winner. The feat deserved a get-together to celebrate in the week end!

In the victory meet at the Bengali's house, most joined with their families. Mukund is alone, having sent his family back to India, in the finals months his stay at America. His wife and two children are in Mysore for fixing a house and next year's schools.

The discussions in the group slowly moved to focus on the win of the boy, an Indian.

"Indians, more in entry and winning many, is not by chance?" A social scientist stressed!

"It is deep in roots; imposed strictures in Sanskrit" He is too sure.

"It is flair and perfection making the difference. It's, evolved attribute!"

He finally concluded.

"Their entry is by passion. We parents push it." Another one articulated,

"We motivate and even polish. We parents have the sparks in us".

The proud patted himself.

The commitment, sacrifices by the Indians for families is a known feature.

One who criticized often on the systems when he landed in USA, lead to unexpected logic? A decade back when he came, his grouse was inefficiency, inertia and hypocrisy in his land.

Later he became perhaps matured, once he climbed in systems roles in Microsoft!

He has observed that the largest systems in the world like, the Indian Railways, Post offices and Revenue offices, still in place; in unimaginable complications.

"Alright. This 'genes theory' and 'propelling wards', is good." He is leading to something more. "For our generation to retain the sparks, we owe to education systems back."

"Most of us are from middle class and lower middle class; studied on free- ships and merit scholarships, from the towns". The successful, in humility shared.

"Without being aware, many influenced us, motivated. Their contribution unsung is, why we are what today!"

His conclusion is," They deserve patting indirectly"

This enthused other, a fond of lyrics in English, while as a student. He didn't want to miss to show off his prowess!

"The other day on an English channel saw an Academician. He was in India, for 3 months study. Finally, he was bowled flat. He admired the system where Shakespeare, Milton, Russell, Wordsworth are alive, and studied even now." Now his stamp of ability came to fore.

"For us, his conclusion lines may sound best; he hinted why we Indians do well in America in English!"

He repeated some of the Academician's words from Bernard Shaw's lament in 'Pygmalion', which later became a movie 'My fair lady'. His memory is intact.

> ....,
> "Oh, why can't the English, learn, to set
> A good example to people whose
> English is painful to your Ears;"
> …...
> "Arabians learn Arabic, with speed of summer lightening,
> The Hebrew' learn it backwards, which is absolutely frightening';"
> ……
> "Well in **America,** they haven't used it for years!" --- George Bernard Shaw.

The end lines induced smiles in the group. That even articulated the emphasis for the Indian boy's win in America; also, it is pride for the first generation of immigrants, with their affinity for their soil; ironically, though being aware that the greatness of Free America, is in assimilating the talents from everywhere!

But for Mukund, it opened an admiration for a person in his life, who in flesh and blood, epitomised the spirit of the English system in India; but he could really notice and applaud its value now!

****

During a visit to my hostel, usually once in a year ritual, my father now a prosperous organic farmer in a village, remembered his old friend, professor Gowda. My father wished for a friendly meet, after many a years of gap. They were classmates in the school in professor's village, practically owned by his father, with hundreds of acres of fertile land. They were close pals, from childhood.

Having decided for it in the evening, we walked along the beds of Kukkanahalli kere, a pond even now maintained well. It is a couple of kilometres from my university hostel, to reach the lavished bungalow of the professor, in Mysore.

"He was emotional right from the beginning, with interest 'in words'. When we were in the final year of high school, suddenly became poet writing many poems."

Father was recollecting his days. "I don't know how he could change to English and why"?

"It seems his father, who does not know English happened to visit Europe, in the team of legislators, was impressed by even children speaking English fluently! The only fond wish of the richest farmer in the district was to hear his son speaking good English! He even brought best tutor from the city to teach in the final year of the school"

"His English lecturers' must have overwhelmed him in the college. I came to know, after a few years, it was his professor who recommended him for a doctoral degree in Cambridge in English"

"But for me, his memoirs are 'poems' written by him in school. His poem, which we you use to rhyme while returning from school, became the best Kannada poem of a young poet. You remember, you studied that in your school days!"

In a short while, both of us are humming rhythmic few lines of our favourite poem with a short distance left to his house. I note only some of the lines in English, with obvious limits of mine. But I really wish that my daughter studies the songs of great poets in Kannada now, when we are planning to settle in Mysore.

Words, dry words, you were once dull and dreary-,
    The chains of the linked letters,
    The moulds of the sounds in utters;
    Pupae to hide in the cosy cocoons,
    Petals to fold in the odourless buds!

    Lo, behold the magic sight of the colourful rainbows -,
    The chains sunk deep into my heart,
    Moulded sounds became soft songs;
    The cocoons opened butterflies to flutter,
    The buds unfolded unto fragrant blooms!

    Oh! The blissful moments witnessed a new awake -,
    The breeze of the air is cool and comfort;
    The shine in the sky is blue and bright;
    The walks of the peacock is steps in grace,
    The sound of the koel is melody in music.

We entered the gate into a European architecture bungalow, leading to an ambience of an English interiors. His wife with a pleasant surprise, is gossiping with father on the sofa of a hall. Whereas the professor is in his study room, for a farewell meet of master degree students with their mentor in poetry. The voices are distinctly audible.

The students though fond of literature as a whole, had influence of prof. Gowda in poetry. It's the emotional aspect, and aesthetic appeal of poetry, which has conquered them.

For many, the harmony of sounds is alluring. The mystery of inspiration is spell- binding for some. The dreamy prefer to cruise on a rainbow, in the supernatural. It signified more than academics for the most.

"Sir, what is your last message to us?" one raised the solemn issue!

The professor who is felicitated as the best critic of English literature in the country, became sober; didn't mince in his talk, though it is passionate in appeal.

"This is what I had vouched to my professor" The 'living encyclopaedia' continued with emphasis.

"You are all **custodians**, to preserve a legacy of the beauty of a language in its splendour. You are carriers to diffuse its delight, moons to reflect the sunshine. Importantly be critical in judgements, to retain its purity."

To dilute the seriousness, one changed the moods.

"Sir, it was a '**delight**' to learn from you. You were '**inspiring**'."

It changed professor's face to one of smiles.

"I am honoured. You used two beautiful words.

It is '**a delight**' because of the sensitivity and grandeur we shared. Though all the branches in literature deal with 'life and nature', the poetry touches gently and is deep in expression. I call it the '**crown of the literature**'."

"Sir, the second one", someone reminded the absent mind!

"'**Inspiring**' because you have studied the best. They are the **gems** of the crown. They shared their, "Recollected emotional moments in tranquillity", with us. Observe the subtle touch you have gained in the last two years. This humanising influence of literature is **cardinal** for me, which you need to spread.

Professor is sounding as if he is only a dedicated moon!

———————————

When the old friends met after many a years, they became school boys. The fair, tall in immaculate suit immediately preferred to remove his coat and tie. Loosening his nerves by a stretch of body, squeezed next to my father.

When my father asked about his son, professor is proud. "He is doing Master's in Economics in America." Later, while getting details about me, he asked in the end.

"Do you write or plan anything in literature?" Probably, to any youth it is same from the passionate!

"I try to write some essays in science subjects. Later I may write short stories." is my humble aspiration.

But he is not satisfied? "Why not poems?"

"Sir, poem writing is difficult, Short stories allow long writings" I confessed my limitations.

"Do you know, the best short story for me is just 6 words, by Hemmingway?"---

"For sale: Baby shoes, never worn"!"

That is a stunner for me! Sensing my embarrassment, my father came to my rescue,

"Gowda, why did you stop writing, in any form or language for that matter?"

The talk is sounding more like a school boys' chat. The elders' are forgetting their age and the two others in the room. The 6 footer professor bending, matched his 5 feet and a few inches friend.

But the bright school boy's face, drooped." When in leisure, deep in my shell I ask myself that question; it even hurts me to note 'what the flow in life' took me to?"

"When my intellect sharpened as critic, I became only a moon to reflect the best. I forgot the **glow** in me. I started feeling, I am even inadequate in front of the band of genius!"

It is a child missing its favourite toy! Perhaps even his wife in all the decades with him, could not have got such a clue from the stalwart husband!

Another boy assuaged his friend," The flashes of ingenuity of the best young poet may be still hiding inside. Remember, even when you talked about something important, the words became rhythmic; it was so natural". Surely it is not to bloat the other! Both know it.

****

On the next day in the weekend at Chicago, Mukund after his breakfast, is thinking about the possible school for the daughter at Mysore. His son being in pre graduation, already trapped for the competition in India. For the eight year daughter, there is at least a few years left, which can trigger the fine arts of his genes.

She is the sole reason for his decision to return to India. He wanted children to belong to his culture! To an argument from wife who is fascinated by the local comforts here, he had finally told. "The children being born here are citizens. Any day they can come back" That had silenced her. His emphatic advice to his wife is to look for a school, more like 'Montessori", where knowledge can thrive with fine arts touch!

He remembered the ambience of his infancy in a lower middle class in the village. The community of ten and odd, struggled to meet ends, though rich in culture.

For the unexpected guests, if a few in number, coffee was made from borrowed milk and powder.

The village river was deceptively still; only when he touched for drinking, the graceful movement was felt. The beautiful flowers on the banks with dyed butterflies shuttling, it was a dream land. In the community, the mothers remembered the children only at the time of food. Otherwise no one knew in which house children are playing?

His wife's voice on the mobile is animated with unusual enthusiasm. "We are very lucky; Shylu could get a seat in the school I was talking!"

The other day wife was all the praise for the school,' Gitanjali'. It is run by best artists in Mysore, two 'kalashri' awardees, one in music –' Karnataka classical' and the other in dance- 'Bharatanatyam'; the third in the trustees is an old man -a 'Sahitya Academy' winner for Kannada literature, with a white beard more like Tagore, that is why the name to the school

'Gitanjali'.

"They are inspiring figures. The school is the best for both in academics and fine-arts. I don't know how Shylu impressed them in her three hours, a personal interaction with them. I never dreamt she could get in ".

****

Back in Mysore, a visit to the schools is his priority. He can't take anything for granted; its future of children.

Also may be a belated acknowledge of the custodian's value, by a visit if he is still alive. The spell- bee episode is still green in him.

After finishing the 'boys' college, the couple with the children entered the premises of 'Gitanjali'. His wife took him to the man watering the lawn, with a towel on his head like the farmers in the fields. When she introduced him as the trustee when he turned, Mukund is aghast.

He remembered the clean shaven, in immaculate suit.

---

2. TIPPU DROP

This narration is neither an adventure nor a bizarre ghost story. But surely it is an account which unexpectedly unfolded, had an unusual twist and even sent shivers in my spine.

The specific place referred to is notorious, infamous and for ones who believe, it is a repository of haunted souls; the womb for hundreds who were pushed to perish or for many more, who are willingly choosing to call an end.

Particularly for Bagaloreans, Nandi hill is one of the nature's stress busters. It is at an altitude of nearly 1500 metres above sea level and is renowned for several centuries of history. The panoramic view of the hills resembles 'the posture of a resting bull' and the name 'Nandi', Lord Siva's mythological carrier, was ascribed to it.

Every king in the region dating from 9th century AD patronised the place with temples and forts. However, attempts for technically impregnable fortification ensued in the 18th century. Tippu Sultan the king of Mysore remembered for the modernisation of warfare in the country, created the celebrated fortress in the hills. It is believed that underground tunnels exist leading to his capital near Mysore, more than 200 kilometres away.

It is a nature's delight for ornithologists, a treat for botanists, a mini Western Ghats in the plains, in that context. From this place originate the rivers Arkavathy, Pennar and Palar, life line for the growth of civilization around. It is a pristine beauty with a man made 35 acres of garden, along with tens of acres of nature's bounty.

Narrations

The snapshot of the overwhelming Nandi hills is breath-taking. The contiguous lesser mounds adjoining provide the contrast, embellishing the splendour of the main hill. The shrub covered slopes, a natural habitat for rare spices of birds, shrouds the hill with a green blanket. The sight from underneath a banyan tree not far away, is refreshing and even stimulating memories of bygone days of my childhood.

Facing directly is the steepest cliff virtually for a few hundreds of meters in a single dip. It is the '**Tippu Drop**' with glazed surface of rocks, having an unusual contour, which is shaped over thousands of years of nature's fury, definitely not man made. The reflection of early morning sunlight from the rocks with least shrubs, beckons its prominent presence amidst the veil of mist and the green hue.

The worst criminals and the evil among prisoners of battles, who were judged to be despicable animals deserving no life, were literally **dropped** in the valley remorselessly. But the spot evokes pity for the ones who are voluntarily throwing away their precious lives. For centuries the spot is an altar for the suicides; a ghastly place.

The inexplicable reason of its choice by the hapless few is still a mystery. Some feel the possibility of the magnetic forces; most deem it, an allure for devils den.

****

The bank of a lake, with the banyan tree is not far away from a small town. It has an ancient temple; a religious retreat for the folks of the nearby villages.

"Sir, looks like you are tired" The coarse voice of a mid-thirties villager, holding a tender coconut breached my day dreams. I felt like an unexpected guest. I called him to share the stone base.

'The lake is visibly shrunk', I wondered' not folk's warmth'!

Though the packed special sandwiches travelled for sixty kilometres, its freshness is intact. It is an unusual taste for him.

"You are visiting after decades", while munching a slice, there is a reaction. "Why so long" and "Tell me why now?"

The issue is ringing in me, before he came.

"Empty your mind. May get clarity, if you are lucky!" a friend had hinted.

'Simple things can be beautiful', I wondered, 'how I managed to ignore!'

"Not many sugarcane fields"? I diverted the talk.

15

He fell silent. "It's water sir. Had seen a lot of trees on slopes, in edges on hill!"

With drooped face sighed. "Gods of rain failed us; for long time."

"Situation bad in town. Most wells have dried."

There is a deep breath. "Water for town, villages is by pump from lake."

But it is for a short time. "We grow now, vegetables and flowers." He sounded optimistic,

"Demand from city has saved us. Money is good."

The snacks and coconut water made some difference in the energy level. I am strolling in the vicinity of temple savouring every moment of replay.

Strange? 'At some places and with friends, re-contact happens instantly?'

'The separation time melts!'

****

On the hills, the feeling is similar. First time I chose to spend the night seeking a new type of experience.

Drinking the chilled water in the yearlong brimming 'Amrut Sarovar' is a delight. The lucid water with naturally added minerals can compare with any other mountain's elixirs. The rain, occasionally down pouring otherwise drizzle did not deter my spirits. As the evening descended the visit to the 'Nanjundeshwara temple' concluded.

It is the space for the real reason of trigger for the visit. The bird's chirpings and the chatters of the monkeys, while returning to night's rest slowly subdued as I re-entered to my night's stay.

Role of paying guest is not new to me. In the afternoon, meeting the owner of the house was a pleasant introduction. The black and white photos on display at the central hall were clear. The ex-military man's conspicuous sturdy frame in the body building competition of services-meet drew more attention from a fragile onlooker.

Captain Arun, with white dhoti and kurta evoked respect from others.

"In initial years from army, in this small place, really missed strangers" He indicated his intents. "So, worked as manager in a lodge here, for some time"

His ease with strangers appears graceful and natural.

"Later, made my spacious home a mini guest house. Demand to tourism went up", he continued, "I am selective, it is only for selected ones. Mostly for recommended."

In the inclement weather, apparently I am alone as the guest.

Military exposures, a natural speaking ability adds to his gregarious nature. While having the evening snacks, a look at the books in the small antique shelf reflected his inclinations. Later while sharing a coffee, he wondered at my simple choice of food for the light dinner.

"Looks like for brains, not for stomach."

He added laughingly, "That's precisely same as mine at sixty plus".

My aim is to have a light early food and more time outside in solitude. I am craving for inspiration, in the open environ, hopefully!

A shower in warm water rejuvenated my spirits. While changing the dress and thinking, suddenly it occurred to me- a possibility of solution from the vastly experienced military man. A good rapport has happened already.

'Why not share scotch, one preserved for long and brought here?'

A surprised look greeted for my offer. The time of dinner appeared odd for him. My repeated requests to share, made him to bring the best glasses.

'How you spend time, looks like its sedate here?' my question was genuine.

"First started gyms in surroundings "Some youth could join army. Most were not knowing how to make it."

"Now, dispute settling takes my spare time", looking at his frame, "my service gun though kept inside, impresses".

With a few sips we opened out more. Meanwhile the veteran has sensed my oddity of hesitancy in my occasional drinking. He has readymade advice –a quote from a philosopher.

"Drink like a 'gentleman', not in excess and without fear".

He added his comment." Not alone". The dinner got delayed, not a much bother me.

"Why you are back again, after years?" My task of initiating the topic looked simpler.

"Looking for 'subject' for my writing" Am fidgeting while confiding my limitation.

"Mr. Arun, its forgotten itch. Time has come for revive"

He laughed with unrestraint. The effect on me is like a splash of waters.

"Thought any incident is an anecdote, and a feeling is a song for a writer"

"Well then," my irritation is obvious,

"Do you have piece of experience so odd, making story with any body's pen?"

He took my challenge seriously, perhaps. He stopped talking and forgetting his own advice is slipping more whiskey, not in a hurry. He is brooding in silence, perhaps drifting to past. The conversations faded. He is a distracted person while eating food also.

Only his continuous sips is bothering me.

Resting on the sofa in the hall lasted for some time. In his face I could see a resolve. Cutting the silence he commanded me,

"Shall we go for a walk?"

I almost volunteered. Hopes of a subject became visible. The bait has worked.

But when he walked into the dining room and brought the unfinished bottle, some uneasiness crept in me.

In silence I followed him. It is a moon light night. But a canopy of moving black clouds frequently creates patches of darkness. The drizzles started with chill creeping in. He is leading me in a specific way though not in a hurry. But strangely his pitch while speaking is low, perhaps didn't want to disturb the solemnity of the ambience. To keep me engaged he is talking casual topics.

"Listen to sounds of animals, night birds"; "Now time zone is not of humans"

The creeks and howls of nocturnal species became distinct and even amplified when we traversed through a crevice surrounded by stones.

After a few furlongs of meandering walk, he signalled to stop.

"You know, some year's meditations made my sensitivity better?"

He is sounding a little mystic now. "The first proof was feeling some oddity from this spot". For me the experience as a whole is unwrapping in unexpected ways; not so pleasant.

Finally, when we rested on a stone, which is an edge near the slope, it is a slight relief.

"We are sitting, where you know?" There is surprise inducing intention.

"it is a few meters from 'Tippu Drop'", horrible one!"

"I don't want to be here in any night" I declared even if it meant meekness.

Ignoring my words he started. He appeared to be in a different spell.

"This is where the worst criminals, the evil among prisoners of battles were dropped literally".

The notion sounded barbaric. "Horrible".

"Yes", he rationalized" Perhaps some are despicable animals deserving no life".

In the moonlight his contorted face looks scary. The fingers are clenched in firm fist.

"Judgement is deceit, a walk on razor edge. If heart melts it can be mercy, otherwise incisive intellect can make it brutal."

That is frightful; long sentence from him sounded an alarm!

He needed a big gulp of raw whiskey and paused.

"The place makes me sad ". He is looking more like his self, "my pity is for who die voluntarily. Commit suicide for centuries".

Luckily for me, situation eased.

Still, for me the place is turning to disgust and even nightmare. The thought of the classmate ending here choked me. All together the eerie feeling dominated creating confusion.

"You asked for subject, you know?"

By that time I no longer tracked it, frankly bothered less about it now.

"Your confusion is true"

In a sober low voice, "Listen again for sounds. From location I showed they fade, distinctly".

He declared," This place is blanket of disturbance!"

Suddenly in the moonlit background a flash of silhouette dashed. It sent shiver in the spine. I missed a few heartbeats.

"What you see and hear may not be unreal"

"Some despairing souls down are craving for deliverance. But surely many, evils holding one-other are thirsty. Even they may be calling more humans to join"

"The animals and birds are more para- normal. In day light also, many don't come here."

The eerie night with the drizzle is no longer chilly. I am feeling to run away from the place.

But timely tap of the old man on by back assured some confidence.

"I know I forced you to this damn experience".

He appeared to handover some special for me, unforgettable!

"Believe me for budding writer tonight will add depth"

"It's time to share an incident now. Not thought will come back again."

When he offered whiskey, I didn't refuse to share.

****

The middle aged Arun, the cottage manager, welcomed a not so happy looking man. The weary stranger in mid-forties after paying the advance in full quietly sneaked into his room without courtesy. His unusual behaviour couldn't escape the observant manager's instinct.

By late evening his worst fears are proving right. The lodger was drinking from the afternoon and even feeble cries were audible near the door. By night, the curiosity no longer remained. It is more of a confirmation for the hospitable soul, peeping through the window. There is a scribbling man exhausted but looking with a resolve.

For the morally upright Samaritan it is a challenge to stop the tragedy. The task became a mission. It is only the question of modality to stop it. He decided to do in his own way.

When the destination was nearing the stranger felt the grip of a strong man.

Exhausted, unable to break the iron grip collapsed on the rocks. Started sobbing and crying. Arun allowed passing of the worst period. When tears dried, the channel got opened.

"My daughter died yesterday. Know it's because of my sins. For that God took her!"

He is emotionally choked up, stammering. Good thing Arun noticed is stranger's belief in God.

"You think God is so cruel. Cool down" He assuaged, "Take deep breaths, relax"

Arun's knowledge about scriptures helped. He started tweaking the weak mind, slowly but steadily.

"You know a famous poet's writing about this human life. It takes many rebirths to reach this. For heaven's sake don't waste it."

"Even if you die how you are sure your sins are forgiven. You may have to face it in next birth."

"For all that, it may be her karmas that took away her. It is your imagination of linking. Remove it"

The persuasive skills dominated. After a long time it had the desired effect.

"You mean, I am not responsible for it"

"Yes. Each one carries his own burden. Others role is only imaginary!"

Life returned on his face. He is even starting to smile.

"Sir, you saved me. I don't know how to thank you. Come to Bangalore. I will give enough money. You need not have to work again." He continued,

"Thank God. I can go back, be normal again"

The word 'normal' sounded the mission's success.

The manager to put an end to notion of guilt for ever, if any residue is left, quoted 'the Christ story', ending with the challenge of Christ 'Throw the stone if you have not sinned'.

"Christ pardoned even Judas. Imagine how big hearted God is!"

"The road robber became sage Valmiki"

"Now you tell what your sins are! 'Confession' may do good to remove your bad feel."

"Sir, I have sinned a lot. I want to share with you, who gave me confidence in life. In future guilt will definitely not affect me" He appeared sure.

The confession became detailed chronicles of deceit, extortion, rape, murder, mafia which startled even the tough nut.

When the commentary of the incident is complete I have forgotten the environment. However, the eerie feeling has subsided. But, the narrator is silent later. The return is easier, only with one point to be told from my side. There is nothing special to make a great story out of this. I don't want to hurt him in the late-night, acknowledging a noble act of saving a man.

After a good night sleep and a sumptuous breakfast, before checkout I told my opinion however unpalatable it is. Arun's red eyes indicated perhaps the sleeplessness, and an overdose. Surprisingly before I started my bike, he came to me and whispered,

"On that night, I returned alone".

---

3. BAHADUR

'The sight of Bahadur into my chamber, with the usual tray of steaming tea with biscuits startled me. I just stood up and froze in gaping. The key man as nicknamed, has resumed his duty, next day after his son's funeral.'

A few incidents of the week is green because of its oddity, bordering disbelief. Sitting on the terrace in my recent retired days, the visible new security, 'a Gurkha' in his usual attire in the front apartment, set off this chronicles of significance.

Ever since the 2 years when the stocky ex-serviceman in fifties is attached to my office, some of his specific traits of duty has not escaped my attention. With his Mongolian breed of high cheek bone and almond shaped eyes, he spoke little, almost bordering aloofness. But the usual grins in the listens, while not missing the eye contact, suggests that he is receptive to interaction.

In the Director speech for the new batch of officers' recruited, I stressed the need of the officer's qualities, as the distinguishing traits needed in a person, quoting his example.

Later, after the unusual incidents, being from the Coorg district which has distinguished pride of a few generals in the army, a curiosity prompted me to know more about this community, 'Gurkhas'. Till then, I was aware of cursory data, but the collated new one is remarkable.

The name comes from 'Gorkha' a hill town in Nepal, under Himalayas. They are presumed to be a 'martial race', because of qualities of Courage, Endurance both mental and physical, Strength, and discipline. The appreciations recorded in the pages about their feat in world wars as fighters under common wealth troops, is astonishing proof for their prowess and signifies their motto and spirit- 'Better to die than a coward'.

Even in the post independent era, Field Marshal Manek Shaw's words, 'If a man says he is not afraid of death, he is either lying or he must be a Gurkha', epitomises the ultimate testimony of them.

The paradox of the 'martial arts' origins, is their peaceful instincts of peasants.

But what transpired in that week is a distinct insight, on the human nature of a person, though commonalities can be an indicator only.

****

The news of the death of an unmarried 28 years captain in BSF, stirred the anguish of the people of the city and the state. The martyr, is the only son of Bahadur, killed in the operations with the terrorists in the border.

There is gloom in the organisation and, most are available on the next day in the official mourning. The dignitaries included the State home minister and Head of Army from the city. The unprecedented flow of people sharing the grief is unheard in the city.

'The sight of Bahadur into my chamber, with the usual tray of steaming tea with biscuits startled me. I just stood up and froze in gaping. The key- man as nicknamed, has resumed his duty, next day after his son's funeral.'

I went to him and shifting the tray from him to the table held his hands. When I stared his hairless, fair skinned face, it is sober, perhaps a façade to cover moist eyes and deepened wrinkles on the coarse face. When I requested him to sit adjacent to me on the sofa, with reluctance he obliged. I am hoping at least a few words from him to relieve his sorrows. But on that day, he betrayed less emotion than his ordinary days, which already is one of to the point.

"We are all sad and share your grief", is my honest submission.

But, the reply to my words is the silence, without cognisable changes in his face. When the pause is becoming confusing, he got up, taking the unused tray in his sturdy hand, acknowledging my words with a nod of head. When he looked at my eyes with his unwavering slanting brown eyes, it is my eye lids which fluttered.

Said, "Thank you, Saab, for your kind words of today and yesterday", and left the room.

It is very difficult even now, to surmise what was going on in his mind and how he was bracing the grief.

After a few days, there is a trickier, but official task for me. It is handing over of a cheque of staggering amount, a small fortune, received from the state government and other organizations.

Sitting in front of me with the cheque on the table, he felt my embarrassment. Without looking at the cheque, when I tried to hand over, he talked with the distinct air of composure in the face, hardly moving lips and teeth while speaking.

"Saab, he died as brave soldier. I am proud of him. We don't need any money on his death. Kindly send it to 'Gurkhas widows' charity fund. We will remember him till our death, for the love he gave us."

I am jittery for my inability even to talk to convince him.

Finally, before leaving the room, looking straight into my eyes in his usual stare, cherishing the dormant pride, said, "For us, Saab, life is a simple dignity"

The diminutive is taller!

I remember the folk song of a tribe, a fighters' clan, near my village. It is a cultural trait inherited and retained, for singing in festive days. Their unique perceptions and feels about life is a surprise.

It is the words when they mourn the warrior's death in wars.

> Mourn him not for his hunted flesh,
> Nor for the beads won in the clash;
> Sing for the pure love he gave you,
> Revel the moments shared with you.

I wonder the spirit of tribes, specially the 'martial clans', who once survived and dominated the wilderness, possibly, only because of pride and fusion of hearts, along with courage and dignity.

---

4. MATURITY

"Remember, emotion saps energy, blinds discretion." The senior auditor's perception is clear to the assistants.

Satish, the middle aged, owning an audit firm of repute is not by chance. His clients know firm's worth and his deputies often experience the reasons for its growth.

The perceptions of the juniors, came out in an evening get-together near the table with filled glasses. It is when other topics ceased and enough time remained for the start of dinner.

From the middle level, who evolved with him for more than a decade had their own specific, though differing attributes. The consensus among them is the professional respect for him with an opinion, 'he is more **matured**'.

"It's his passion for the subject. Look his sparkling eyes when he discusses. Its passion adding his degrees, some international. That's the decisive edge." – The one who switched earlier firm for the sake of learning more, is emphatic.

"I like his way of taking chances. Almost call adventurist. He embraces the projects, others don't dare to lift. Fiddles even the failed one's', - one who loves secure zone, commented.

"Look his obsession for Sherlock homes. It is his brilliance to notice small things. He dissects with logic, puts together for decisions. – it's his intellectual acumen man!"

"Can sit for hours with same focus; what an endurance? This is the prime!" -One who often wavered after long hours!

""c'mon, cut it. Many have all these. He sits with U for your troubles as if it is his problem. It's his empathy, motivating all"

"More than others his orderliness, I feel, sense of time mattering. Am telling his unique mental organisation!" – The one who is disorderly missing schedules lamented implicitly.

"For me it is his silence. He doesn't argue unnecessarily, even when someone spikes. He is unruffled by triggers"

When dinner approached, the aged one, who believed on age for maturity than others concluded – "He is fast learner, its accumulated attitudes".

Though he is convinced, looking at him none explicitly endorsed.

****

May be all are true in different degrees. Every one's opinion is either blow up of their own strength or weakness, that too when they were high with spirits inside. In reality, it is a mixture of some, which made things possible. Satish is aware that he is not a superman!

Some lines in his dairy of college days hints his evolving nature. It was after an intense experience in the class room---

'The old professor who respected teaching to religious level left his sandals and stepped on the dais, as usual. In the middle of the lecture, the messenger with a telegram note arrived and handed over the message. The scholar folded the note after glancing and continued the lecture, from where he had paused, without any hiccup of emotion.'

Only later, the students through the messenger got the news. It was about death of his old father in his village.

The note in his diary mentions-

'Today's experience is unbelievable. Throws light on my long time dilemmas. 'What can be more provocative than father's death? I have respects for him for erudite and humility. Today, saw a man who has mastered an art; he is an embodiment of control of mind. Let him be the guiding spirit, in my predicaments in life!'

The note ended with a quote:-

'A matured is one who can be objective, even when stirred emotionally – Roosevelt.'

****

His wife, within a few months after marriage has noticed his tolerable oddities. She had studied psychology as major, and has keen observations.

Satish's elder sister, whom he considered as mother, once had thrown light about him.

"He was emotional boy till 10, when the mother died. After a few years, there is a vague feeling for me- he deemed emotion as futile distraction"

After acquaintance, the couple had even discussed some issues which they differed.

In the discussions, both were clear about one thing - the zone is at personal level, only with a few.

For wife it is, –

"Emotion flows from the heart; it can't confuse like intellect. Involuntary emotion is positive and it's one's strength. Is not it beautiful to be one's own self? Does it not add a flair?"

"I agree with you; it is soothing and pleasant." His argument is logical,

"But differ in some".

"Emotion is not the cause, it is effect from thought. The spontaneity you feel, is short time in response. But its free expression and carrying away by it, is the concern!"

"Are not the emotional, act in haste and regret in leisure? The issue is to restrain it, once you know its source."

She is happy that it is not absent in him; it is saddling of emotion, his aim.

In one argument she is emphatic.

"It's emotion that keeps families and relations together, which triggers selflessness and sacrifice". His is a little different concept. "It's not emotion, but the 'integrity' that binds and holds'"

Whether it is 'sensitivity', 'passion', 'emotion' or the 'integrity'- they are a happy family.

****

When the daughter is born and later for a few years, there is definite observable signs of cracks in his conviction. "He started spending more time with her, becoming attached. Daughter brought mellifluous tones. Any of her achievements is amplified in the inner circle. Once she had a cut on the forehead which needed stitching, he was about to swoon in the hospital."

****

But the real litmus test is when the daughter is getting married. His sister remarked," I don't know how he takes separation that too she is settling at abroad?"

For Satish as the marriage approached, spare time is becoming haunting moments of memoirs. But his composure during the ceremony surprised wife and sisters.

The dim lights and the vacant chairs in the marriage hall hinted the end of ceremonies. The tired Auditor sitting on the chair is feeling relieved, after hectic function. He is even feeling a pleasing sense of triumph.

'In the imposing waves when mortals can be ruffled, has shown courage of detachment.'

When the final call for the flight was made, hither too composed daughter came and held his hand gently squeezing. The tender hand with fresh mehndi imprints conveyed every feeling. It signified thanks giving for all that the doting father showered in her life time. In those precious moments of transition in her life, the vibes acknowledged and assured gratitude.

Involuntarily, driven by an urge, she touched the mole on his forehead and gently caressed, like what she used to do as a child. He felt a drop of her 'warm tear', a pearl on his hand.

> Tears, idle tears, I know not what they mean,
> Tears from the depth of some divine despair,
> Rise in the heart and gather to the eye"
> Tennyson.

His eyes inundated with copious flow.

---

5. BEAUTIFUL PEOPLE

"In the body of flesh and bones, I am wondering about the '**soul**' aspect?"

The face of the 70 plus external evaluator, has a peaceful glow. Till then it was corrugated wrinkles on the forehead, with dissecting eyes of shrink. For the doctoral candidate Nandu, in philosophy, the changed development is unexpected. Till then he thought, everything will be a smooth flow.

"Always the 'Plato's Republic', fascinates me for it's anytime relevance. You have dissected and analysed aptly." The initial words was pleasant; an encouraging sign.

Focussed study for two years in the thesis is in the final clearance; but it is anxious moments in the last hurdle.

"You have touched the subject in all five facets of philosophy. But I feel it's a scientific study of a philosophy subject; that's my concern!"

When he saw the worried, he encouraged. "Nothing is lost! Add two new papers to your main?" There is a sign of relief in Nandu's face.

"Plato's 'Apology' is the tribute for his emotion; a heart stirring poetic prose. It is a great piece in the world literature! A poignant narration of his mentor Socrates's end, gladly accepting the poison, refusing to seek an apology and ending for his convictions. Make a paper on the 'human Plato', who was present when his mentor consumed the deadly hemlock."

"Otherwise you will miss something in your life!"

"Second is in conclusion part, where you have sprinkled quotes of the best; there is scope to fill the 'human spirit', the wonder in the flow of the world."

"Philosophy is not stagnant or dead. Write a personal feel on some **beautiful people,** you have met, 'philosophers of first waters'. Then you will like the philosophy, 'love of wisdom'; it will prove, it is alive till man lives."

"Look for them, feel them."

****

Nandu understood the 'crux'. His one need is to make a paper, about the common men who are special, from true experiences in his life.

He pondered a few instances. Curiously, most are green experiences in his college days!

****

It was the days in the college hostel.

'The mid -night tea is common in the exam days. The café near the hostel is open full night. On a night of heavy rain, a rural bus from a village dropped a helpless worried couple, carrying a child with high fever. The hospital they need to rush was a kilometre away, unknown to them.

Spontaneously one from our group, snatched an umbrella from another, proceeded towards the hospital taking them and comforting. For us 'the next day morn's exam' is the gravity.'

Ponnappa, who volunteered was a typical hardly opening purse for spends. But his act on that night, and later known fact of parting of sizable money he received from the poor father, prodded soul search in us. It was an eye opener for avoiding hasty presumptions about others.

In the evening after a matinee show, we friends were having tea and biscuits in a hotel, usually referred to as, 'Irani hotel'. After finishing, in the customary way left some coins as 'tips'. Before we left the door, the waiter of 13 to 14 years came back and returned the coins, "Sir, I am paid for my work by the hotel! It is not correct to take money".

For his attitude we were stunned. Our first reaction was," Why the boy is so impractical?"

But within a few minutes' walk, we realised and it was a sheer admiration for his spirit.

A fracture for my father, needed my rushing in the first available morning bus to the town. I lived in the outskirts of Bangalore. Getting early morning auto to reach the connecting city bus 2 kilometres away was a problem. Luckily, I could meet a known auto driver in the night, and explained the issue and got his assurance of availability in the early morning near my room.

In the morn it was heavy down pour of rains, and still the driver managed to come. He was unusually in a hurry and returned without taking money from me. "I will take it later."

When I returned, I met the head shaven driver, and understood that on the same mid night he had admitted his father in coma at a hospital in the area.

I reflected sometime in disbelief. It was a case of commitment and integrity, unimaginable! Finally, I had saluted him.

———————

A religious function was performed by my close friend's family. In the leisure of life in the cultural city Mysore, such occasions of participation is common. About 150 people joined in the rituals to be followed by a traditional lunch on banana leaves, on the floor. The function hall was a small one, which could cater to about 70 to 80 in the dining hall. Everything appeared in control, till the first batch's lunch was coming to an end.

Sensing some arguments near the hand wash in the back, I rushed. It was an argument between the cooking and the cleaning staff, finally the latter walking out of the hall. It was moments of panic and confusion, a helpless embarrassing situation for the family. With the first batch finishing and next waiting, there was not much time to think; it was only to act!

One gracious lady of mid-fifties, a guest in her gorgeous Mysore silk saree, called two of us, and asked to get the big carry bags meant for collecting used leaves. In no time, she started picking the used banana leaves and filling the bags. That encouraged us to speed up and finish cleaning, along with her.

She almost ordered us not to eat in the second batch, till all finish food.

Later, we learnt that she is a chief gynaecologist, in Chicago on her vacation.

We had seen many volunteers helping in the occasions. This was something spontaneous without any pretexts, hinting at the basic trait of a person. It was simplicity and leadership quality, even motivating others to do!

It was my return in vacation from my uncle's place at Lucknow, for a journey of almost 2 plus days to Bangalore, by train. In the afternoon when I boarded the train, at temperatures of 40 plus, it was sweating and annoyance at the unruly crowd.

When I squeezed in my reserved seat, the cabin being occupied by a tribal looking family from Rajastan, it was more irritation. The group for a religious trip, were in lunch, squatting everywhere with 3 to 4 children in boisterous mood; they even offered their primitive looking food to share.

To avoid the noise and chaos I shifted to top birth, and remembered my aunt's words. "You are carrying costly gifts back".

The two brimming suitcases was carrying fancied wishes of many, who had lavished money for getting priced local articles. It made me to carry the most valued material things in my life.

"Be careful in these trains. Lot of theft will be there in some belts. Don't believe anyone in the cabin!"

As the evening progressed, I was feeling weak and sensed a raise in temperature in the body. I remember vaguely what happened in that night, when I was in the start of a typhoid bout.

"Some milk was put into my mouth, a continuous feed in spoon; someone or other was tending cold cloth on my forehead and chest, throughout the night. It was till reaching Hyderabad. They had managed from me, a phone number of my friend at Hyderabad written in a diary. I was in a delirious state, it seems.

I came to my senses in a hospital, with drips, with my worried friend in front. When I saw the suitcases in the corner of the room it was relief for me.

On that day, I had realised the inner culture of uncouth rural folk, as an inherent quality. Whenever I remember the incident, I become speechless.

———————

As the captain of illustrious Basket Ball team of the college, I had moral responsibility to groom the next ones. It is to keep the team best in the colleges of the university. The absence of a potential new comer on the field, after a few weeks of practice, forced me to enter his room on a Sunday afternoon in the hostel.

"Why you stopped. You can be a star in the university team in 2 years". With many a radio sets opened, with a soldering iron in hand, he was cool to respond.

"I also feel it. But my priorities changed. If not helping my poor family, at least I should support myself. That is best in situation now." He continued," My hobby is helping me now".

I had nothing to reply for a twenty years athletic boy.

It was sheer spirit of owning the responsibility and carrying on.

His conviction and focus took me to my first year in the college, when I was in a worst situation in college times.

My national merit scholarship was held up due to some official clarifications, in my first year of college. The clerk in the office said," We don't know when it comes. Now already it is mid- year. But I am sure that you will get it in the next year beginning with this year's also. It has to move to Delhi and back, from the university office and come back to us. There is a lot of procedures."

It was a shatter for my academics. I was totally in disarray. "His fees and hostel expenses is covered, in my bright son's scholarship"; I remembered the happy proud face of the school teacher father talking to our neighbours in the town. Somehow he had managed my first few months requirement from his meagre savings.

It was my assistant professor who noticed my perplexity and asked the cause with a few days left to pay the annual fees. After some pause, "You are lucky. One of my friends helps bright poor students. I am sure I can recommend your case to him. You can collect money for your expenditure from me, every month, till you get your scholarship. For this year's fees you meet me tomorrow." I was in tears.

After a few months I wanted to meet the big heart who is supporting me.

"You can't. Because he believes that his left hand should not know what his right hand gives." It was only in the next year I came to know somehow from others, that it was he himself giving it.

He is a Muslim strongly believing that he should not take the returns on his forced NSC investments, in his salary. When I fell on his feet in his house, with tears in profuse, he lifted me and told," Get me a Gold medal in the course, that's your return".

What act can I say is nobler?

For Nandu, it is becoming difficult to confine in the bounds of his paper. He had not realised the list can be so exhaustive. There are so many, some compassionate 'magnanimous', some 'simplest' even in high statures, some with spirit of 'independence' under deterring situations, many who conduct with 'a trust' as virtue, in life. He realised that he had just taken it granted for, as a possibility.

Reluctantly, when he intended to short close the memoirs of '**a few beautiful ones**,' he couldn't forget the meet of his 'green team' with the renowned now, 'Salumara Thimmakka'- now a 'National Citizen Awardee', and on whose name some environment programs are run in USA.

A casual labourer in a quarry, in a village near Bangalore, had married a cattle herder, but with no children for years. Both deciding to grow 'Banyan trees' in view of missing children, in decades planted and tended 384 banyan trees, along a 4 kilometres stretch in a highway near the village. They planted the samplings in the suited seasons, fenced them with thorny bushes, and carried water for 4 kilometres to feed the young saplings. Today the value is more than 1.5 crores!

Leaving apart the value, which is not what they wished or intended, the only alive Thimmakka in her old age now, is aspiring and motivating the youth in the village, for greenery and perineal water resources.

When our team met the wrinkled graceful rustic in her village, sitting on a stone bench in front of the modest house in the village, involuntarily we sat on the ground below her. Chewing the powdered betel nuts with the leaves, in the teeth-less mouth, she looked beautiful. Curiously there is no advices from her.

Frankly there is no need for it. Her monumental work with her husband, reminds her commitment if we keep our conscious open and if our eyes can see. "Initially we did it to overcome the grief of not having children. Later, we realised in the quarry area more are required. So we continued till it was possible", sufficed their intent.

No wonder, she is the inspiring vitality for many groups in and outside the country.

****

When Nandu is placing the punched pages in the compiled dossiers, he felt the unusual heaviness in them, like his heart felt while writing. He glanced at the quote in the end, which is one of them in the conclusion of his main thesis; luckily for him, the wise aged evaluator had hinted it.

"To be a philosopher is not merely to have subtle thoughts, nor even to found a school, but so to love wisdom as to live according to its dictates, a life of Simplicity, Independence, Magnanimity and Trust."

--- Thoreau.

6. STINKING SANDALS

Shambu, the teenage nephew is in a relaxed mood. He was reading a newspaper in the late morning with a coffee, during his days of vacation in the uncle's house in a town.

The moment his uncle rushed back from his routines in a hired Ambassador taxi, Shambu knew it must be important.

"Get ready, we have to rush to the city", sounded serious. His uncle who is the chairman of the municipal board in the town, doesn't mess his words.

But the words," you learn more in life, if you visit graveyards and ICUs" sounded ominous, for what is in store in the journey.

The uncle's annoyance is not without reason. The death of his old mentor is not unexpected, but the information he got from a common friend is delayed by a couple of hours.

"They forgot their town and people". His reference is to mentor's sons who are prosperously settled in the city now.

It is the mentor, who noticing the bright boy in the cursed colony, had inspired and moulded him. "A worthy lamp not only dispels darkness in the surroundings, shall kindle more to shine"; that was the advice to his uncle and other bright youth of the town.

The mentor is a part of the success story of the town, which became prosperous from an insignificant village. When he was MLC in the parliament for many a terms, he had sincerely tried, his best.

"I want to end here, destination so near", the words of the old man a few years back had hinted at the town graveyard near his agricultural fields. But later, he had to reluctantly move to the city, selling everything. The pressure was from the sons, who are professional real estate developers at Bangalore.

The uncle does not want to miss the last homage. When they reached the house at the city, surprisingly body is already in transit to a crematorium. Also it is not at the one nearby, but to one which is at the farther end of the city.

It is a great relief at least to have the last glimpse, a token of gratitude.

"Why they didn't wait for the people from the town?" his query to a friend is logical. "So many, whom he has helped are coming in buses."

"They didn't want to make a big propaganda. Also, thought the body may **start smelling**".

"Why, it is not even a few hours."

"Why did they bring here, when they have one nearby?" The answer from the friend is more curious!

"I heard from the younger one. It seems here hot water facility with clean rooms are available. Also, I heard,

"We can get free services here with the help of the local councillor, who is a father's friend.'"

When they returned, it is late night. Shambu, is hungry and removing his shoes and sacks, rushed inside to the bathroom to wash himself, the usual routine after visiting a grave yard.

"Aunty, I am hungry.'"

"Call your uncle also, I know he would not have eaten anything from the morning". Shambu's aunt from kitchen responded.

She continued her advice to the nephew, shouting," Before you go to bed, bring the shoes and sacks inside, even if it **smells!**"

When Shambu went outside the house, the uncle is still in the daze, of losing mentor and more so because of the day's happenings, sitting on a stone bench. With his slanted head looking at the tall coconut tree, is murmuring himself.

"As night falls, we don't forget to keep even 'stinking sandals' inside."

7. TM. (Transcendental Meditation)

[With respects to Maharishi, Sri Mahesh Yogi]

Narrator: - 25 years youth, from the lower middle class;

Bright in a small town, both during his time at IIT & now in Designs at a firm of repute, has cognised-"Nature's impartiality to shower best seeds everywhere'. His prime concern now, is to slide his family to middle class; it's fierce competition among equals.

Period: In 90's, but relevant for any time.

Scenes: Starts with 1, to flow later.

Scene1: It is in the subsidised canteen, where many from other departments will be present.

Scene 1

On that day in the canteen, it was less talk and slow eating, unusual for me.

'Is anything fallen from sky?"- Some observant remarked. Realised it's for me. Shrugging from thoughts," It is not a bother, but curious!" I threw a surprise.

"I notice boss has changed a lot recently", shared my thoughts.

"For 'good' or 'bad'?"

"'Both perhaps'! Real Truth is, has become smart with focus." I Continued,

"He doesn't shout, but it's difficult to confuse him",' I shared my amusement!

One from my group peaks technically in the late evenings; Uses other times for pastime - reading, crosswords, Sudoku and puzzles,

"True, am loosing rhythm. He is imposing timings", he reinforced Boss's oddity.

The boss's perception is tricky, a new found theory.

"Finish work in time. Any slog beyond, means either of two", was not messing.

"Am loading more, means should pay more. Worst, it implies a wrong plan from me". The other was the real concern,

"You may be inefficient" – Ominous threat for the team!

But my thought is different! "He is more relaxed; even hums a few tunes often; Packs off at correct time".

"Throat problem for his fat talkative wife? Or else, lucky man trapped interesting one?"

One from personnel dept., which recruits, then tracks beautiful one's reacted, to his bent.

"For months now, no rush for us from lunch. Boss, spends extra half an hour in closed cabin."

"You mean he sleeps or eats slowly". Negating it I clarified,

"That's what curious I told! With a placard - 'don't disturb, am in TM', shuts his eyes; comes out relaxed-better than sleep."

"What is TM?" The nicknamed 'speedy', agitated always, reacted. But to his dismay was ignored.

"Coincidence! My senior today was telling," the salesman wondered.

"He told -Two weeks tour in a month; "Anywhere to meet all types", 'Really stressful'. Am now practising TM for de-stress,"

"Didn't tell me what's TM", a little irritated now; always wants things fast.

"It is Transcendental Meditation".

"Never heard that"- The Market man's real surprise, who always believes in Ads.

Sale's one rationalised," They are low key and mute. Seems, they feel- with good product, interested come to them"

"Wish such products are here", marketing guy stared at the design team.

"I want to join"- An instant reaction. The word 'meditation' enthused one with religious bent. His guilt is ignoring of the rituals. But it is emphatic words.

"I will arrange a decent vehicle, on Saturday afternoon. If, many agree to visit." the personnel man with control over transport is hospitable, at no cost for him!

****

It is 2 hours' time of handling, for an Australian Instructor, in pure white loose clothing, head and face shaven. Sober to the point, with incredible ease, fluency, focus and confidence. We were dozen and odd.

"Try yourself. Here is simple method, which works"- the smile shrouds a hint of challenge.

"Wise teacher with experiments of decades in solitude at Himalayas, with wisdom of early generations offers you this. His intents, only to help us"

He moved to questions from us, almost immediately. But there is no hurry in his demeanour.

"Is it religious?" the religious one wanted 'yes' for a 'Hindu'; but is disappointed.

"No, am a Christian, continue to be one."

The beard man's worry is," Should we shave?"

"No force of any type. No rituals." He continued," Only we want, sparing your time- twice a day, twenty minutes each, anywhere."

"Any equipment or accessories?" The one tuned to Gym culture intervened.

"Your body is the equipment. TM is the tool to influence mind".

With no queries in queue, there was a personal touch,

"Look. Beatles found a new dimension in music; hippies discovered better community living, without drugs."

I felt he is smart to touch our psyche, by 'Quoting examples of TM's efficacy on West's popular!'

"Any interesting results here, in your camp?" I quipped with a tease.

"From the feedback, it seems it is effective." Sounded optimistic," Even batches from unusual have enrolled already in TM. One from 'elected reps' in politics, other is 'inmates of a prison'"

The silence of 'the speedy', was surprising for his patience,

"Tell me sir, is it for 'relaxation' or for 'focusing". In a breezy speed, he shot out. His need was for 'both'.

"This is the most beautiful question"; the face of 'the speedy' lit for his apt nail, hit though late.

"Remember the secret of men of success, and who are happy, 'well,' is the use of synthetic coins, with these two faces."

"The whole purpose of TM is to learn the art of symbiosis of 'relaxation and concentration'. It's for success in life, whatever one does."

That was irresistible free offer I felt, till he added. It's one month's salary as course fee!

"Nothing is free in the world, except two. One, the mother's love", he paused.

"And", I was curious!

"It's advices of many, though not interested in you, shower it freely". Ensuing laugh was good beginning.

"Some decisions in life, "Which subject to pursue?", "To finalise a partner", "Choice of profession" are 'decisive moments"."

They are 'short moments', making huge difference in life; most with 'no comebacks'."

"Why not this be such 'vital moments ', unexpected, least risky. I again repeat, no compulsion here and it is voluntary." There was cautious note at the end.

"Remember it's not panacea. It's for your empowerment; to face life'; to be practical".

****

For the interested ten, first session of 3 hours began within a week. It is a 'feel good' interaction with the specific course teacher. He compiled our personal attributes like- inclinations, habits, conditions of physical and psyche, aspirations, present concerns bothering. In the general program, where candidates can be from different places, it meant also to create an ease in the group; anyway that is not needed for our cohesive team. In different coloured papers the data is recorded to tag progress in the program.

The small talk opened up some peep into TM. It looked they are less esoteric, more realistic. But during discussions on a 'Syllable', it became a bit abstract.

"Each one of you is discrete and special, though everyone is made of same 5 fundamental constituents, in different degrees. It's this beauty in nature along with your genetics, defines your identity"

It's believed that at the time of 'big bang', when 'universe was created', the first sound was monosyllable, 'om'. It pervades everywhere.

Small thing like 'genes', is decisive factor in human's nature. 'Om' and 'genes' are 'small beautiful things'.

The tool of TM is 'simple 'monosyllable', special each one." Many got disappointed, though not disillusioned.

"Who chooses that, and how?"- One in the group was curious.

That's the significance of the experienced linage of teachers. We respect the gentle souls for sharing their methods of experiments.

"What it does", was the next query.

"By continuous chanting in silence, it induces vibrations in you, creating new sensations." As you practice, slowly it can become an awakening of some specific nodes in you".

"Sir, isn't spiritual issues you are talking".

"No, I want to stress only practical aspects"

"The awakening am talking is to help you to discover 'natural modes'".

The teacher seemed to cut our curiosity, and concluded.

"Believe me, this is something which is to be practiced and felt" and "Not to be intellectually analysed, prematurely."

"In the next week on an auspicious day, its vital moments in the program.", "Our senior teacher will initiate, I repeat, specific to each, syllable – **Mantra**".

****

The crucial day, arrived. The process is simple to capture. - Initiation of the syllable, in person by the senior teacher.

Next, is the first practice in solitude, under the watchful eyes of him!

The ambience of the activities in a big hall with ample of air, and less light of evening twilight, has sobering effect. It is the silence and the dignity with the reverence shown by the ones who conducted, adding gravity for the occasion.

It is no time to analyse, discuss or explain- only to feel, that too in personal level, in silence.

———————

"I felt it's rebirth with the mantra", an enthusiastic shared; "Its first time I felt myself"; the one in tears after first practice. For some it had no effect.

For me some memorable moments happened.

One was while sitting for 'initiation'. The photo of the teacher, a miniscule figure in the vast back of inimitable Himalayas, took me to my visit of the place of grandeur, purity and serenity. A place where individual's significance fades - The enormity of Nature makes anyone humble. In the reflection of sunlight, I had felt moments of melting into surroundings.

The second one, which was much deeper, happened during the first practice session, reclining to the wall. Repeating of the mantra, with closed eyes continued. Slowly breath became smooth movements. Later I had to adjust my posture to become straighter, less inclining, for deeper breaths.

As the practice continued longer, the feel of the place and time, started fading. I felt drifting to some other beautiful moments of infancy.

It was the pious ambience of the village hall, where I used to go with my mother. As the musical concerts with the melodious singing prolonged, I use to end up sleeping with my head on one of her laps.

When the teacher woke me up I am in dazed state of spell, perhaps from deep sleep, a forgotten habit! Later in the evening detailing a few finer aspects of methods followed. Possible distractions and finer traps are cautioned.

We were told to follow the process, twice a day for twenty minutes each. The follow up includes a sharing of group's experiences every fortnight for three months, a voluntary option.

****

In one months' time, in the group a few interesting incidences happened.

One was with religious man, who discovered suddenly, chanting a special verse for 108 times, takes 20 minutes. Arguing not a coincidence, switched over to it. The second one was with an academician facing adaptability problem in our firm. Within a few weeks identified that the lack of siesta after lunch as his problem. His hour long sleep had the same placard like my boss, giving mystical touch, to his undisturbed snoring sometimes, for intruders.

In the last session after three months, where most of the initiated present, it is smiles and ease. When the sober Australian instructor distributed the coloured papers for the feedback, he sounds more approachable.

The 'speedy' but appearing 'slow' now, has a special request to the instructor, with a mischievous smile,

"I have a request. When you compile the results, don't combine ours with 'politicians' and 'jail mates'. We are yet to evolve!" Visibly he is the most cheerful in the group.

****

Now after 2 years, I confess it's more of 'inside experience', a personal one. – May depend on culture, attitude and perceptions!

The intensity of first experience never happened, but most of times it is a drifting soothe, with exception of slipping to sleep sometimes. But surely after sessions, senses including eyes, ears were sharp, with deep breathing following for a long time.

Am not a religious buff or inclined to it. Equally am not prone to analyse, 'divinity' or 'spiritual' issues, with other priorities.

The sole reasons for my try with TM is, personal empowerment for better success and to feel myself. It worked for me to expectations! Some questions, like 'how?' and 'why?' still remains.

When my senior cousin, a psychologist from US visited, his theory seems plausible. - A case of 'self-hypnosis or auto- hypnosis!' Though, initially some ponderings happened, specifically about- the choice of 'Syllable' and experiments by the refined minds for hundreds of years, soon I realise the circuitous nature of analysis.

Perhaps is wisdom gained during its practice for two years- to think of its benefits only! For anyone who shows interest in TM, my honest suggestion is

"Please try it".

---

8. MUSICAL MOMENTS

[Inspired by Dr. Madhu Nandhuri,
the renowned Sitarist]

In the low lit party hall, it is cheerful air. For the members in the get-together, it is lively moments - one of sharing and sprightly. The music in the back ground in a low pitch, blended with grace.

For the seventy plus old, any good music is 'Pure' and 'beautiful' – like his white clad Khadi. Initially in his life, it was a curiosity which prompted to peep into it, but after decades became an obsession. His exploration altered his perception to one of mystical awe - Comparable to 'deep waters' and 'open air'.

With the entry of a gracious couple into the hall in the twilight age of end sixties, moving in with a poise of classical dancers, there is a soft recall of his wife.

Wife's analysis proved riddle sometimes, as their life shared mutual interests. It was revelations and educative, in the flow.

"Music is reflection of Nature"; endowed with a keen intuition, she had hinted for his wonder on 'music's spread in the life'.

"The ragas evolved with humans as 'inseparable essence' ".

Her words, especially when she talked about her favourite, appeared like mixing of tunes. With respectful gratitude she had remarked, "The ragas were perfected by genius, in higher dimensions"

His other curious observation in the musical concerts, was the 'reciprocal nature' of tunes. The maestros, could induce the emotions in the audience, by touching their subconscious!

In the college he had studied, though not felt, John Dryden's ballad, 'The power of music", wherein the king Alexander will be swayed through different moods, by the master of music, Timotheus -

"Master saw the madness rise...,

Changed his hand and checked his pride" --- John Dryden.

_____

Slowly, the initial excitement of togetherness is subsiding. The exquisite food quietening the initial appetite, the members are settling to their comfort modes- conversing, some even slipping into gossips, with cursory eating and cool drinks.

For many, the silence is a soothing though in an alert mood; when curious unusual, can be stimulating. It can open up of trapped signals or even can induce new perceptions. The ambience is proving 'the Timotheus effect', at the subconscious level.

The visual flashes of the Silhouettes, of the gracious couple is inquisitive, who are a blend like a song with music. Slowly, their unrestrained affinity is turning into deeper dents, with the seeping background music, swaying to one of 'melody in fusion'.

The specific classical rendering in sitar, his favourite, is a pleasant surprise, making the meet meaningful.

The master of the sitar has gone another step higher by exploring of finer aspects of a link –'moods with feelings' and 'time breaks of the day', in an innovative reveal. The weaving of 'ten slots' of times of the day with definitive ragas, and correlating to moods- an exceptional concept had stunned him, in the first listen.

The stirring perfection with fidelity on the CD depicts the eight facets of human feels-"Serenity, vibrancy, delight, fantasy, anxiety, exuberance, melancholy and the solace', with unique artistic mastery. Their correspondence with the ten phases of the day, is amazing.

But his undoubted choice is, the heart touching tunes, of ones which 'Rhyme with softened heart, mellowed by any deep feels including sorrows'. The melody of this genre can be in a wide range, of a tinge to soul stirring.

The pathos of dooms and tragic, plunge the prey to despair, but in less intensities of feel, can pervade and sweep all human relations- Delicate pains for the sensitive, dissonance in rhythm and hurts in partings.

****

[The old lady resting on his broad chest with his left arm circling her firmly, hinted moments of fears for separation.]

[Mystical, with acceptance of impending end: Suggestive of Night slot]

It is a very rare gesture from the inexpressive husband! For a middle aged lady, husband holding her palms with a gentle squeeze is surprising. Hence it meant more than the words.

The present life is a routine, purposeless, drifting to boredom. Even it had decayed to signs of broodings of missed imaginary possible. But the life is disturbed recently.

"Amma, why don't you come here for a couple of years?" It was a persuading request," It will be great to have you when the grandchild arrives."

The request of son from abroad stirred things, to set her ponderings -

'All my life was slogging. Short of money in the beginning, later sacrifice for children- Spending time mostly in the kitchen. None asked what I wanted? Endured like an ox on yoke. I need fresh air at this time - A change of place with new meaning. Why not this becomes a chance to prove my value to the husband, who has taken me for a grant?'

But today's act of husband has - an expression of heart, the inner feels. It is an anxiety for missing her, even a sense of helpless request. Implicit in stares are rare gestures of gratitude for all she did. 'Before you leave, we shall go to market".

The husband's words of care" You don't have many good saris", is touching.

Together it is an expression of gratitude, which she had longed. Inexplicably, the share of burdens endured felt worthy. Contentment enveloped her, ensuing deep breaths - a feel of gladness, fulfilment.

The gentle shake un-wrapped the folds, initially for the husband and now for the wife! "I have decided not to go", it is a firm resolve, "Anyway daughter-in-law's parents are ready to be with them" sealed the issue.

It is a pleasant surprise for an overwhelming emotion. When she stared deeply into his eyes, she saw the reflection of dim light in rainbow colours.

———————

[They were sitting straight, standstill with their heads a little bent backwards, and resting on the top cushion of chairs. But their hands were in glue- The ten minutes seemed eternal.]

For the young couple of a few years' marriage, the news of divorce of a friend is disturbing, even shocking. All had begun with a minor innocuous rift. This news of the friend inducing ruffles of anxiety, is sounding a cautious bugle for the young ones.

"I don't want kids now. I have a great job, some things to prove in my life". It is a clash of freedom and identity vs. emotional need. " We need a wonderful child to glow our life and bring a new meaning" is his sincere plea.

It has become simmering ego clash! Though the surface is frozen ice of both being adamant, the undercurrents has undeniable silent concerns.

But the air in the evening caused soul searching.

The morn was anxiety; the evening bared insensitivity. The dormant guilt surfaced after awareness. Acknowledging it, their hands twined with relief – for a rekindled trust.

[An evening: Rejuvenation with joy]

———————————

[His hands gently caressed the ringlets of the part of white hair locks, even the sensitive ear lobe. Nothing mattered now.]

For the waiter standing in the hall, evening work is light with fewer crowds. The earlobes, his obsession reminded the thrilling short times he spends with the young wife in the village.

"We will take some loans and purchase some cows also". Father's words of wisdom,

"Two acres of wet land can keep us happy. Why you want city life?" had not deterred. The request of the young wife, couldn't turn the misplaced priorities.

The dazzle of bright lights is blinding him. It is a fantasy of 'city can make miracles'! Today, he cannot avoid the flash of the wife's pleading eyes, hinting the inside hurt, while he returns to city. In the maddening buzz and the crowd of the city, he is feeling alone without any identity.

After moments of wavering, there is an emphatic nod in the shake of his head. A feel of hopes of different rejoin, is overpowering.

[Afternoon: fantasy of warm feels of the beloved]

[The old man bent to kiss the lady of grace, when they stood up to leave. The teenage wished it was on the fragile lips. The tender kiss was on the wrinkled cheek flowing with droplets].

The teenage daughter rushed for the terrace in a hurry. She wants a free space and time for the talk on mobile. The vibrancy of the active young has its own tones. The trigger of the evening is excitable enough to spur her.

The gentle kiss, the seal of love has reminded the boyfriend. The moments she spent with him alone were adventurous and exhilarating. His fondness fascinates her. But why he should be close to other girls?

She had not taken his calls for months now. She desperately needed to make one now.

[Morning: splendour of vibrancy]

When the teenage daughter left to the terrace, her parents are driven to shuttle in time capsule - A visit to great Sun temple, an adventure decades back.

Long back, the visit was an eye-opener, with the postures of carnal passion carved in stones; the temple has sanctified the coitus to a religious level. For the conservatives it was a shocking revelation, though hither to it was subconscious possible. The visuals which 'Kama sutra' only worded, had invigorated their marital life. Together they explored and felt the bliss of nature's vital secrets.

Now, with dilutions and inability to fathom its depth, the intimate mating has become intermittent casuals, drifting to boredom. Today with the hint that **'affinity is mind-set, not of age',** there is a dawn of awareness-Exploring the mystiques need not stop or loose the charm! Both decided for a revisit to the place, earliest.

[Delightful day: soak up in the sunshine]

In the background music, it is the last one in the garland, locus of the ripened.

[Late night: a surrender seeking solace]
For him it is the feel of the soul, seeking the bliss of the end. It's a total devotional surrender.

When the couple who held hypnotic spell on some are leaving, Old man cannot avoid the memories of his departed wife, a virtuoso in music.

Her voice had inspired him to finer levels. Now, her thoughts are haunting him to emotional heights.

"Music when the soft voices die,
Vibrates in the memory…,

So thy thoughts, when though art gone"; P.B.Shelly.

For many, the stolen musical moments of the blissful couple was magical alum particles, precipitating dust to clear turbidity.

But, after sublime moments of togetherness, the enigmatic couple is worried and are inevitably parting. They know: Dodging spouses and children, is not easy for the next meet!

---

9. Dearest Delight

"Not seen you so much engrossed for years", Wife's words sounded true.

"Tomorrow, is a tricky challenge; a type never faced till now."

The professor of philosophy wondered – To teach swimming to ones in pool is fine; to lure one to pool! He was jittery, but wife's words," remember how important it can be'; the timely caution forced the focus.

The challenge was to enrol enough for a course in 'philosophy', an optional subject, for engineering students.

Impressing by lofty ways is equally hard for an intelligent or for a fool! Fool fails to notice, the intelligent ignores. Definitely they are not fools: too sharp. Perhaps, one can disagree your views, but sincerity only can touch them, at least to listen.

The pin-hole view, needs right things with elegance. Right things is choice from plenty, but elegance? It can only be by mix with inspiring words of the best of minds!

****

The voice of the speaker has a genuine touch of concern. He wants to hit the nail in the beginning itself.

"Do you know how many youth in the city ended their life last year? You have mourned a few from your own college.

The listeners, who are all final year students from the different streams of engineering became quiet.

"Am not preaching here, want to share my anguish, want to see you are better prepared, to face the world."

"Look at the immediate tension you are carrying? Campus selection, study at abroad, good grades in fierce competition - all are sapping you". The irony is it is paralyzing you and for most, not allowing to perform to potential. My worry is that it may become a trend for your life!"

"Sir, we are on the hook, inescapable reality it is!"

"I know, but you are here to consider enrolling for the optional subject. Remember, this subject is not for passing the exam. If cultivated, it can change your life. Small thing can make big difference!"

"This year is not the end, rather is beginning for adjustment problems in jobs, handling unemployment, frequent change of jobs and later perhaps trying to avoid divorces. Strange is, many are not able to handle even success"

"Sir, you are going to fast forward mode. Let me save myself for the day"

There was a pleading in the voice." Am aware not to push panic button or talk crazy! Its impending realities and a way perhaps, to cope up in life"

"You sound like some, psychological councillor?"

"Am trying to avoid them for you guys, now and later also"

It is turning to become an interesting duel!

Having created an air of acceptability, he stretched confidently. Now the usual voice of the professor of Philosophy- a subject of his **Dearest Delight**, surfaced.

"My friends', seniors in Software industry who pick U guys, even in campus have a point" All ears became receptive, after the words, 'software' and 'campus selection'.

"We prefer balanced ones to intelligent eccentrics", they can give better output and suited for group tasks". He continued," They know test results are indicative, can be deceptive- so may ask our views also"

Suddenly, the Issue carried more gravity than anticipated, in the practical sense!

Writing the word in calligraphy style," **philosophy'** on the black board, paused.

"The word literally means, "Love of Wisdom", most beautiful!"

Someone not getting carried away," Do you want us to bring beads for the class to chant?"

"Sorry, it is not religion or spiritual". It is mother of all ideas in the world, by the best minds in humans.

To stress the point, he said;" Even the Software evolved by philosophers in - languages, methodology and processes."

"We shall discuss that when I hint relation between science and philosophy"

"Now, want to focus on tangible benefits. Some already we talked"

"The main argument many pose - philosophy has no 'survival value'. True, it may not give material prosperity, but look if it can provide a 'value' to your survival. Science can give us knowledge and power, philosophy can herald wisdom and freedom of mind."

"It makes you better humans. That is biggest asset", "Touch your heart, is it not what you want?"

"The next ones are curious and they are nurtured by undercurrents. Philosophy encourages questioning, cajoling you to explore meaningfully. Philosophy treads where others don't dare!"

"It can stir creativity, insight and free will."

"The significant thing is, it sharpens thinking on 'Methods of Thinking' itself. - The spiralling effect can be explosive"

"Sir, sounds great. But I don't understand"

"Well, it's like 'self-looking into itself'. May be confusing you more".

It is like, as if someone says" Often I talk to myself, I need expert advice".

Looking at raised eye brows,

"Don't worry, suggest you join the course, we shall discuss and feel the finer aspects"

Professor appears mystical, even while he delicately cut off discussion after showing a beautiful carrot! It is not yet over.

"If attitude is cultivated, it helps you to become efficient in 'any learning'." That sounds trickiest unfathomable theory?

The room is relaxed and for some points perplexed too.

"Summarising the benefits," continued in his class room style," It relaxes to tap your potential, makes you better humans, empowers to face the harsh world, improves efficiency in learning." Laughingly added 'can get a campus selection'. Glancing on the note, the absent minded," Sorry, I forgot to mention. The close ally of philosophy is 'sense of humour'- It helps to carry loads with smiles"

The professor after the prime issues, paused in pondering.

A pragmatic made his job easier." It is impressive, some enigmatic; but tell us, what is philosophy, and supposed methods of teaching- sir, please not in abstractions to go over our heads."

"You put it rightly, this is an introductory course for exposition, meant to cultivate for long term". Instead of talking what it is, I prefer to link it with what you are already familiar?"

Philosophy is 'mother of all sciences. It puts a framework, provides guidelines and creates an environment for evolvement."

"As already told, many of the principles of software were speculated even 50 years back- The Languages, methods and processes. The best minds who guide by creating the paths are identified as philosophers. They march in unexplored territory. After intense hypothesis & concepts, they hand over the baton of ideas to another energetic group, to perfect methods for practical utility. They are of science genre."

"Thus philosophy looks at Nature and natural things, propounding possible theories, call it-speculates. The theories are dissected, interpreted by analytical ways to be useful - by science. Even standardisation is done for efficient ways of productivity".

"So, Philosophy creates a science. But Wiseman doesn't sit on ivory tower! He keeps an eye on advancement."

"Invariably, when the new path is needed, it creates new theories to hold hands of science." If you think of any subject you have studied, the new progress is again initiated by philosophy, validated by science. And it's a continuous dynamic process".

"In the example, to make it easier for your background, I confined to 'software evolution'. The science can be any framework including social science, political science, mathematics, even philosophy itself!"

****

"As for the methods of the course, am glad I am empowered to choose", "I prefer for the studies some selected frame works in the evolution from different sciences."

"The next is more curious. We shall study the theories by looking at the life of philosophers who made them possible; here is what the human touch, I was hinting comes"

"We shall think with them in the background they lived, share their ideas along with anxieties, perplexity; shall laugh with them and even cry. We realise in the end they are beautiful ones, yet simple like you and me"

A few I mention may showcase what is in store; they may baffle or even amuse!

"One who is deemed as greatest ever, while in ponderings doesn't hear wife's abuses. When she pours bucketful water remarks," Earlier thunder, now rain comes.""

"One proposes the best social order till now, thousands of years back. The king who sponsored the project suddenly realises that it implies the abdication of throne to philosophers. To avoid hanging, the philosopher has to run away"

"An expert in abstract subject is fluent both in English and German, and teaches at England and Germany. On a rainy day after one hour in a class he realises he is talking in other language. When he points, "Why none of you told me", gets a reply," It doesn't matter".

"A sceptical pupil to test truth of his teacher's claims hides coins under the bed. The genuine teacher, gets burning sensations on the bed while trying to sleep"

"To test the conviction of a philosopher, who adores the attitude of acceptance of happiness and grief equally, the apathy as a virtue, the king breaks his leg. The philosopher smiles in his pain, true to his preach.

Their stories and life's, basically suggest that problems we are facing is not new and existed eternally. The stories enthuse and amuse, the theories inspire and the attitudes with sense of humour lightens. Overall the beautiful people and their philosophy soften us."

What shall we conclude?

The course is a pin hole, for a possibility of panoramic view later. In the chaotic life of exploded knowledge, philosophy can induce and sustain human values. More importantly it can make life bearable and meaningful.

10. GUILT

Raghu's affinity for the grandmother is unique; not only for the affection aspect, it's for her fascination for the latest gadgets.

She even forces Raghu's father, to make her grandson own the costly devices. The teenager shares some of the down-loads, from you- tube and Apps, with the curious keen observer. Covered with sagging lids, her small eyes brighten with a stretch, for the unusual interesting.

Raghu's latest download, captivated not only the grandmother, but all in the home: father, mother and elder sister Leela. It's because the curious few minutes of video clip, matched the common context in the house. The sister has joined the family for her first child birth, with a month plus gestation, remaining now.

Ever since the grand daughter's re-entry in the new role, the home has a breeze, with lively fresh air. It is a trigger for the old, to shed her sedate stance of counting beads, to one of mercurial activity. After the child birth, it will be grandmother's fondly waited moments of responsibility.

****

The video shots is an excerpt from the medical research results, a gripping moments, displaying the developed child's antics in the womb. Though haze, in the contrast in the blend, the movements are clear for the focussed eyes. Floating in the womb in the liquids, with the attached umbilical cord swaying, the child is in excited mood, even clapping with observable grins, for an unspecified stimulus.

The spectacle shared many a times, silenced all with an awe of disbelief. It excited the grandma, most among all the five.

It is an evidence, endorsement for her long believed notions in' Mahabharata' episodes.

"I knew their intuitions were stronger than science. Only others' realise now"'. "Someday they will prove the possibility of multiple embryos, preserved in a pot, to become hundred siblings; 'conception' is possible without contact, already proved! This is only beginning".

To emphasise, she revisited the episode, now more confidently, about 'Abhimanyu' during his last days in the womb - son of Arjun and nephew of Sri Krishna'.

Krishna, in the late evening chat with his niece with the child inside her, describes about a troop formation, supposed to be impregnable; even if penetrated seldom one can come out. It's referred to by the legendary name -, 'Chakravyuh'. [Circular strategy].

His commentary highlighted the finer aspects of the methods to infiltrate to dislodge the enemy formation. In the surrounding silence with the keen sensitivity of para normal hearing, Krishna will be listening the response of the child from the womb. But, by the time he explains how to come out from the formation, the child is in deep sleep.

The great tragedy later in the war is, how 'Abhimanyu' who knows how to enter but not for the return, succumbs gallantly, before causing unprecedented havoc in the enemies.

"Not only the child is not dumb and deaf in the womb, the growth, both physical and mental depends on the mother, from the beginning." The domain expanded now, for reinforcing more beliefs of hers.

From the day the granddaughter conceived, the phone bill had sky rocketed. It was repeated advices. Other than what to eat, it was the psychological issues of keeping cool, to be happy by visiting for the flowers in the gardens, to listen soft music. Instruction was to avoid sorrows, cruelty in TV serials, even terrors which can induce fears.

"Don't read the thrillers" – is a restraint for the favourites of Leela.

"Your thoughts will affect the child in growth, so be cautious", is her strong advice.

Finally, grandma's seize is broken by Raghu.

"Don't tell me, the child's brain is only by that". She has ready reply.

"No, but can make a huge difference, both for brains and physical!"

But inexplicably to all, there is a pause in the flow and her face even drooped with some pondering. Recovering, "Sometimes I don't know, it is the '**Nature's inclines**' or '**God's will**', that prevails".

"So, 'Nature' is different from 'God'? Raghu's teasing quip, is common for grandma. Only he has the licence to talk like that.

"'God' created 'Nature' with some rules. He gave intelligence to humans. It's for humans to carry ON meaningfully. May be, even 'He' cannot change 'His' own rules."

It is unbelievable, that grandmother is accepting limitation of 'God', despite her strong faith! Everyone knows, it will be a curious recall from her dossiers of past, but this time may be unusual, because of her initial comments. Even father's chair, did a slide towards the grandma seat. He does not want to miss this.

It was, 'when the grandma, was a young house wife of a clerk in a small town, with two school going children.'

****

The town is usual like others, except for its temple of 'Hanuman'. It is inside a huge quadrangle, with bounty of trees surrounding. An ideal place for monkeys to thrive and prosper if enough 'food' and 'water' is there. Water is from the small pond and the food, voluntary offers from the devotees, who suddenly become aware of the existence of 'monkeys' among them; even deem a representative of the idol in the temple, 'Hanuman' - the wisest of all, with a boon of no 'death', with supernatural powers endowed to him when he was young. It was by the deities who are symbols of earth, water, fire, air and sky, the ubiquitous sentries of 'nature'.

The monkeys' are benign; only in exceptional cases they attack, if provoked. The sight of accepting the 'bananas' and the 'groundnuts' from the hands of devotees is a thrill for everyone, perhaps more than while offering prayers to the idol. There, it is solemnity to seek blessings.

The onus of conducting the rituals, is on a priest. He could sustain the devotion of growing devotees for decades, like earlier ones, with total submission in his task. What the people are insensitive, or blissfully unaware is his mundane ordeals, to sustain a decent living for his family, with meagre earnings.

The trust is headed now by an ambitious leader, an obdurate opportunist in the town, whose forefathers built the temple along with donating the golden ornaments to decorate the idol. His grouse is the missed treasure which he could have inherited, if the predecessors were wise to retain.

At least now, if a couple antique valued ornaments can come to his hands, it can make difference in his political growth. The only thorn in the way is the respected priest. His notion is clear,' they belong to me'.

Someday, even that happened. The most painful times in the life of the priest is when he accepted the money from the wealthy, to conduct his only daughter's marriage. It is in exchange for his silence when idol was less decorated by a few ornaments.

It is a dream come true for the greedy family, even hailed by teenage daughter who also got married on the same day, as the priest's daughter, by coincidence. Even knowing about the source for her golden glitters on her body during her wedding and the part of sizable dowry, she did not even visit the temple.

For the priest's daughter, a sensitive, the reality dawned by a subtle hint by mother, before leaving for spouse's place. Only, the 'self- pity' of financial constraints could rationalise the action for the family. Soon in the flow of times all forgot it.

But it came back with deeper dent when the daughter conceived. The silent tones lurking, echoed back with amplification. 'The pangs of conscience', pricked their hearts, more so for the sensitive daughter, now more sensitized in the days of pregnancy. That blew out of bounds for all in the family, when she came to town for her delivery, at her 3rd month after conception.

Now, the 'self-pity' failing to douse the act, soon decayed to repentance, with the daughter seeking amends for the misdeed. She is spending most of her leisure in tending the monkeys in the quadrangle, initially with devotion, which later turned to affection and pity for the helpless creatures. They are, reps of the image of the deity, in flesh and blood.

****

Grandma's narrative abilities, always fascinates Raghu.

"We were living in the rented portion, in the same compound of that leader. We knew their family well. The priest wife was my close friend".

The grandson couldn't control, when grandma is digressing the end. He felt she is making it dramatic. Till now, there is nothing exceptional!

"Then what happened".

"On an eventful day, we visited the maternity hospital. It was strange coincidence again. Both girls delivered on the same day, like their marriage date".

"When we entered one room, leader's family, was rejoicing the healthy heir, distributing sweet to all."

"But, the other one was with 'an undeveloped brain', having the features of a monkey."

11. DEBATE

In the dynamics of life, the present is absorbed for essentials. Even the memorable moments are obscured in the flux. Such indelible moments usually link to youth times and friends. May be because of, "Better tuning of chords and carefree age, where any oddity is implicitly accepted!"

Some imprints can become touching and endure long. Such need just a trigger to relive again. That is what happened for a close friend of Ponnappa, with an agonising trigger!

****

'After the mid -night tea during exam days, it was raining heavily. A bus from the village dropped a helpless perplexed couple, carrying a child with high fever. The hospital they mentioned, not known to them, was a kilometre away. One, spontaneously snatched an umbrella from other, took them to hospital. For us the next day morn's exam is the gravity.'

Ponnappa, who volunteered was a typical who hardly opened purse for spends. But his act on that night, later known fact of parting of sizable money he received from the poor father, prodded soul search in us.

****

The following narration is a rare flashback of weeks, where I got associated for helping the roommate. It is for preparing material for a 'debate'. A sudden development. Slowly the occasion forged friendship, understandings with mutual respect.

On that specific day, the usually the restrained showed signs of his hurts. There is a hint of personal feels mixing up.

****

"Gods die young for many", his first lines in the debate has startled me. **"For me, God is not born".**
'This is not in what we had compiled!' I thought. But I am happy for the impact it created. Till now, it was words, rhetoric otherwise - Now it's heart pouring out. Hall became silent. Behind his pulsing voice, there is depth with conviction.

In the room a few weeks earlier, "please help me to prepare' had moved me. It is in earnest. Till then he had not asked for any support. His pastime - 'spending evening hours with slum children', has earned my respect.

"Good dissecting ability, editor of college magazine?" it looked like grease. But it did bloat my ego. His choice is **'not needed'** in the subject, for the inter-university finals; it is contentious, prone for emotions. My initial reaction is,' difficult to side you"

"Relevance of religion and need for its resurgence"

"Why can't you do, thinking you are me?' is tricky and challenging.

"Not the challenge, subject is too serious!" I even stressed "difficult for your view!"

"Think you are organizing the subject for the debate, without mixing emotion."

"OK. On one condition, don't mix my name in this".

I am afraid of getting branded as 'rebel'. He agreed readily and I have faith in his integrity. "This is my best chance. Debate, you know, more freedom," he is sure, "My mission is for changes"

————————

Strangely, the hours of hard work we did in the library, is educating- a learning which I have slotted - 'later in life'. It is a window to peep for the words of scholars, quotes of best, and feel of philosophers, critics, so beautiful, vast; but it is becoming a herculean effort, to contain in the frame.

My strategy," Tell me what you want in the end. We will fix that and come backwards", only saved us. But in the study I am drifting many a times, while luckily Ponnappa's focus is intact.

The difference is in our perception for the task- its stimulating exercise for me; will be vital minutes of heart throbs for him. Finally, the job is turning as compilation of his feels, with reflects of fine human minds to suit it, in a cogent way. My role is a detached observation, though curious.

****

"My friends' glorified religions by quotes:

"All roads to same end", "the branches of big tree",
"Repeated quotes for long, stale!"

"Our purpose is relook, for its utility now." He is candid.

It is more like a pleading.

"A few issues about religion shocks me.

The first is - Religion is birth basis, not by any conviction."

While penning the lines, I am feeling the truth in it. Am I not a Hindu, and continue now, because of chance of birth?

"This is amusing – 'What my forefather did is right'"

"The next is claim of superiority, without glance at others".

I question myself about it - My knowledge is skin deep about my religion itself!

"The worst - Most disown negatives of religion!'
Perhaps, fear for realities."

"How can we ignore some havoc, it has caused for millions for centuries?"

"The worst, humanity will not forgive is 'wars!"

"More people died to preserve, spread religion than epidemics. Cultures were erased, innocents hounded and persecuted"

Then, is an emotional choke unexpected.

"The caste system! Someone's grandfather carried 'excrete' on his head; his father, only cleans toilets. This is for life times. This is true for thousands-" Why only them?""

.......""It is difficult to surmise what it feels, for them?"

There is an apparent regain of composure.

"Worse than the physically carrying or cleaning, it is the notion of karmas, put into their minds-We deserve only that'? It is a perverted analysis of 'karmas'; It is religion which backs it indirectly.

What followed is what we have planned - structured, cogent and logical arguments. It is organised with end written first.

"What is religion? – We need a closer look at vital things which make religion. They are "Myths & rituals, morality & ethics and truth which I name spirituality".

"Do you know difference between Vedas and Upanishads?"- The query when sipping coffee in the break from the library had caught me unprepared. For me they are sanctified scriptures unquestionable and needs maturity of age to fathom!

"I had heard some Wiseman talking about it", He continued," with our efforts now, I can say one thing-Looks like, Vedas are myths & rituals. Upanishad is truth seeking". "It seems many westerners are fascinated and even endorse Upanishads as truth of truths"

"Myths evolved to explain the unknown, with limits to grasp the enormity, - So' belief' was needed."

"The 'myths' needed actions for support. – 'rituals provided them'."

"Thus, they are for social reasons - To feel secure, to vent out anxieties; a group psyche for social reasons, to contain fears, to satisfy curiosity."

"'Astrology' and 'palmistry', a few myths, are fond hopes. They cannot be proved. Rare coincidence is glorified, most others are ignored."

I wonder about his natural flair to fill life to words and his abilities in memory.

Then it is the slot for morals and ethics.

"My friends' prided - "'the by-products of religion, -ethics and moral issues' Good! No argument for relating to social factors."

"But vital issue is, with other limits of religion, is it the best way?"

"Historically pagans, now no-religion groups, do they lack morals or ethics?"

"What are 'morals' and 'ethics'?"

"It is tolerance for Hindus, spread of happiness for Buddha, a Compassion for Jesus, Nonviolence for Jains, Nietze claimed it was bravery of strong, and the

soft hearted Plato declared – Effective harmony for whole. Note the list can be endless. Why?"

"There can be hundred definitions, because the 'ethics' and 'morals' are just interpretations."

"Well you may argue, if I am agreeing their value in the society, and if religion can provide it, what's the fuss?"

"The tragedy is the claim of ownership by religions. - "ours is the best.""

The focus switched to 'Spiritualism". While discussing, he had shown, intuition and clarity on the issues.

"Are Buddha, Buddhism and Buddhists' same? When I looked confused he had shared his argument."

"Buddha's quest was not for a religion. It was to feel the true happiness; to know the root cause of 'grief' and to overcome it. It was a way to lead life, culminating in Liberation, when the Nature (Dammam) is correctly experienced. For many queries of his disciples, his answer was silence."

"His next generation inspired by his ideas and methods spread it, but adding their own interpretations. They were influenced by their earlier cultures. This spread continued and Buddhism evolved with distortions, amendments. Scores of different sects, conflicting in some ways emerged, with affiliations to Buddha's name."

"Most Buddhists are now, generations who were born for ones who adhered to different sects of Buddhism.

Invariably, they embrace it by birth or for social reasons, not for the affiliation to principles. Like other religions!"

"That is the truth of any religion. The source is fountainhead and pure in the beginning, like our Ganga river at Himalayas. Later - distortions, interpretations, contortions and dilutions creep in, degenerating to become polluted like Ganga River at Banaras."

"What I call Spiritualism is the experience 'of' the node by a few. It implies 'at any time'. Even now for any one it may be possible to feel what Buddha experienced, what Christ felt or what the rishis of Upanishads time perceived."

Ponnappa's explanation sounded logical, brilliant.

"Claim of spirituality by religion is peculiar. At the root, the inspiring souls who are fountainhead of later religions, finest and beautiful minds, must have felt dual aspects.

- **The silence of space and**
- **The feel of inside serenity."**

"But followed in mass, with cultural infusions, distortions, without the finer minds to cognise original beauty, the significance fades. After Centuries they degenerate becoming' myths' and 'rituals'."

"My cardinal point is, the need to delete spiritualism from religion. It is confusing the issue for the common man. One thinks that he is moving

towards 'truth', by following rituals and myths. Let this domain of 'truth' be left for real seekers of truth."

It is a slice of time for conclusions.

"Well, with all these what to conclude?"

"The religion is hyped mix of myths, rituals, morals and ethics; all are nothing but, 'social aspects'".

"Relevance of religions, doubtless - is just 'social order', only social order; nothing else".

"Well, religion has proved inefficient; disastrous. Like the stinking 'Thames in England, sometimes back' and present 'Ganga River ''at its flow. The irony is most minds may accept the pollution of rivers, but fail to fathom the same about religion 'Possibly, by fear-, individual and collective."

"Thus the crucial need now is for creating a new social order, pushing religions to insignificance where they deservingly belong."

"With prosperity, peace, growth of knowledge and health_ boom using science, there can be less collective and individual fears- The 'myths' and 'rituals' hopefully loose flavour. The new order may usher a system where justice, equality, happiness and freedom prevail."

"Creating the new order is challenge for the social scientists and philosophers. Let us remember what the great philosopher Plato 2500 years back declared,"

"Religion is a noble lie propagated by philosophic elite to ensure social order"

"The need is to accept religions as' a lie' first, and to displace it by a nobler social order".

****

Now, looking back after nearly two decades,

It is a spirited effort by teenage minds, an age where any organised institutions choke; an irritant becomes frustration, systems sound insensitive. Also, it is when the depth of enormity of issues is intangible; the insignificance of ripples in the inertia is ignored. But I had sensed the seeds in an evolving soul which can 'stir', if not 'shake', the accepted norms in the environment.

Today's newspaper report which
triggered all, is a shocker.

It is difficult to surmise what he went through in his life? He was a humanist with hopes and optimism, selfless sensitive, not harmful, but seeking a new order. The end of a turbulent soul by the same system, which he dreamed to improve and change for the better, is biggest paradox and irony.

---

12. THE SECRET OF
THE CELLAR

"Everything will be fine, nothing to worry" The words of the lady doctor, "It may happen in a week" brought cheers to all.

It is a routine panic visit again. The richest man in the town and around, has even engaged a midwife to be present in the house. The lady doctor is any way nearby in the small town!

When the first son is expected, the mixed emotions of 'elation' with 'anxiety' is not strange; it is indeed a rare event for all. A few married daughters of the house with some of their children are already present in the house.

Husband's fat belly could somehow hide churnings in the stomach, but his rare black face, is showing enough of his concern. His mother has observed the unusual jitter, with the delivery days approaching.

"What if a girl is born like me & with the brain of the mother?" Finally he confided his queer concern, with his mother. Lata's cultural value is counted less here!

In a short span after Latha's marriage, all including the married daughters of the house have the same opinion-"

the girl is cultured, but without a business mind"! Which is a hallmark of his family.

His worry is not unfounded. His father's ordeal in the life was the marriages of the daughters, dark and bulky. Luckily, poor ambitious youth were plenty in his community. His second motto in marrying a white beauty is to avoid that seen hazard.

****

How an adorable, refined flower from a village, became a fancy of the house, is curious!

"I want to marry a beautiful girl, even without dowry!" the hesitant practiced words of the son shook the father. That is the most unexpected and unheard in the house! The father switched Off the 12 band murphy radio, to which he is listening and paused. The amazed mother overhearing at the kitchen, could not avoid joining in the hall. The big hall with four fans became mute.

The embarrassed son, soon left in a hurry for parents' to discuss. He did his part. When he stepped out of the house, a romantic song from a touring tent theatre is filling the air.

The confused father is staring at the frames, hung above the embedded show case, as if to share his dilemma, needing an advice. Soon he is sure that the people within the display of black and white photos in the frames with brown tints and a painting of the couple, the origin of legacy, will not agree.

But when he looked at his wife, the daughter of a wealthy, he surely feeling, though belated- 'I wish I had same guts.' Though every generation had cherished the same idea, this is the first explicit say. Also, now he has felt the conviction of his son; after all it is the changed times now. With no other choice left, he finally endorsed his son's fancied inclination: it is a rare gesture of magnanimity!

****

Latha is the first daughter of a small merchant near a temple in a village. She is delicate like the flowers he sells, having the fragrance of sandal sticks. The coconuts and the fruits he sells, are the genuine offers of the pilgrims for the divine surrender. The background music from the temple invariably spreads to the entire village. But the benevolent God has gifted many a children to the family, instead of prosperity. Not that they are not a happy lot.

Their main asset is a contentment in less, and discipline in the life.

When the unexpected alliance is brokered, it has become a conflict for the family; more so for the young girl. A glimmer of hope for mitigating the financial misery for the family is in the offing. She is too young to surmise the hidden equations in the world. She is any time ready to cope with the hardships in any modest family in her life. Now, the notion of sacrifice for her siblings swaying her.

On an evening, her parents presented an invaluable gift to the rich man's hands, with a mix of a 'tearful note' and 'a happiness of hope'. There is an earnest plead, in their glistening eyes to take care of the precious gift they are presenting.

> She's the bloom of our floral yards,
> Filling our hearts with odorous spreads,
> Swaying, dancing, with the moving winds,
> Sure, she is lovely; isn't she lovely!
>
> In the cheers of evening twilights,
> Our humble present is for your delights,
> Possess, protect in your watchful ward,
> For, she's precious; isn't she precious!

The girl became the pride possession in the new family - a path break fortune of a different kind, slowly subsuming to the new environ. The melodious voice singing the religious tunes is becoming a regular feature in the neighbour's houses.

Occasionally, she now remembered the touching last moments in parents' home. Her mute parents had heard the matured words. -"Want to light the other candles of the house, to glow at better places'".

In a short time the smart girl could fathom the ways of the new house. Her husband's fascination for the physical charm is evident. But she is going through the process of adapting fast, accepting the realities. For the one who has faced tougher hardships, these routines here are simple. Initially the members of family, have the feel of pride in her inclusion to family; for their own reasons.

After a few months an additional responsibility is expected from her.

It is the supportive supervision of the tasks in the cellar. The cellar is spacious, divided into different zones, separated by cheap sheets. It is looking of archaic in make. The house had changes over decades, with exotic furniture of 'red sanders' and modern gadgets in flourish. Here, less ventilation and dim natural light is disturbing. Even the electric bulbs of 40 watts at a few places is not sufficient.

A cursory look suggests the stocking of valuables like TVs, fans, Radios and tape-recorders they sell, in one of their shops. Some rooms, are dedicated to black marketing stuff to avoid official's eyes. But most space, is meant for speculative store for seasonal commodities. A team of lady labourers, on need basis, work in the backyards for cleaning the pulses and other grains. They are packed in the gunny bags and stored inside. It is the use of available space in a best way.

The entry to the store is well fortified, with entry restrictions. Only close knit two labourers can enter into it. One is a fifty year man and the second is, his blue eyed nephew. They load and unload the commodities, whenever, three wheelers and even bullock carts are used.

Latha's new additional job is to support her mother in law, for the supervision of the operations in the cellar. For the aged mother in law, it is a great relief to see that Latha could handle the task, so that she can spend more time in the house. But she is not ready to handover the kitchen, as it is the symbol of the head of the family.

What is curious for Latha is, the stairs leading to the cellar from the bed room of in laws! Inside the cellar, she has seen a closed room, under the bed room. It has a lock, possibly not opened recently, from the cellar side.

She is wondering many a times, 'is it for unaccounted cash, gold and documents of properties'? A lot of confiscated papers from the poor defaulted farmers, is common in the house. Even she has seen the gasping father in law, occasionally going down the stairs.

Her surmises are true to certain extent. The room in the down is by legacy, has vaults embedded to the walls storing the valuables. Even now it is the trove for the fortunes the family holds. Earlier it was protection from the thieves, now it is a hide for the tax sleuths.

Even now, the tangible treasure is physically present. But in the time wraps, some intangibles which the room and the cellar had witnessed and infamous for, are shrouded.

The shrieks of obdurate loan takers when tortured, has faded. The sounds of the bangles and the moans while mating, are absorbed by the walls. Along with the greed for money, the earlier ones had other indulgences. The escapades of dissatisfied in the house is also an inherited legacy.

The smell of the mix of sweats in the intense sharing and the aroma of the intoxicating liquors, however have drifted away through the sparse ventilations of the cellar.

****

The naming ceremony of the grand son, with all the religious fervour is apt with the family grandeur. The God inexplicably has heard the concerns of the family, especially of the husband. The brown boy child is the 'cynosure' of the evening, ornamented lavishly with gold.

"Thank God, though late the heir has arrived", is the voice of the grandfather, contented now.

It has been four years now after the marriage. However all choose to forget a few year's turmoil of Latha?

"Must be problem with the girl, let us show her to doctor!"

"I tested both. Though the sperm count is less, it may improve over time with medicines and no need of panic", the doctor had declared.

"Let them go to pilgrimage". One sister had hoped.

When the time endured reached 3 years, it was panic. The overheard in-laws words, had shattered her. "Why not we go for the second marriage",

"No, let us wait some more time", had postponed it.

It is the most unexpected rude shock. The conflict now is worse than the one she had faced at the time of her marriage. Now she felt like kicking herself. Earlier one was a decision taken for a noble cause! Now, it is becoming desperate helplessness, with no choice in the looking. The people look cruel, insensitive. Now she hated these people with disgust.

****

"The child looks exactly like the grandfather, same long nose and brightness". The conceit in the face of grandfather is obvious.

When the child started crying, sensing the need, the mother in law advised for a breast feed. Covering with her sari, the proud mother offered a suckling for the child. Glancing in the hall, she focussed on her parents and sisters from the village. The eyes of the now relatively prosperous from the new business, signalled 'thanks giving'.

When the naughty child suddenly sucked the nipples with force, she cannot avoid remembering something.

When Latha with a wry smile, stared at the eyes of the child, she could feel the blue tint in them!

---

13. THE FLOWER IN THE SCHOOL

His tender daughter, picked up an unusual gift from the heap of birthday presents.

It is a beautifully bound book, with gold coloured emboss of letters- DIARY. He couldn't hide the pleasant surprise. Later, resting on the siesta chair, felt the precious letters, by the gentle touch on them. His face became soft, the fingers delicate. The word became dearer. The stillness of silence and the fresh breeze carrying the scents of jasmine flower, had a lulling effect. It was a rare strange feel, after a hectic day in the office, later in the evening for the party. The loosening in the nerves amidst weariness. In the soothing of Nature's feathers, remembered some of the lines he had jotted long back.

"In hours of weariness, sensitive sweet,
Feel in blood and feel along heart...
For tranquil restoration"
                                   --- Wordsworth.

In the school days, he never thought such a pastime of diary writing existed. The white paper was a precious commodity, which was allowed only from 7th standard. Using the slate was a dreary feel. It had encouraged him to remember lessons by heart and to do calculations in mind. The next stage was using brown paper with pencil.

When the city cousin, showed his precious belong, he too longed for one. Back from vacation pestered his mother, the only one whom he can! It was not easy to influence her who did a balancing act to run the show. Though his pleadings failed, his drooped dull face did the trick.

Yielding finally, she stitched one from the carefully preserved white sheets. The unanswered sheets from the exam booklets meant a different thing for a school teacher's family. She was the only one in the system, who wanted more exams, less answered, definitely not by her children.

Having owned a crude diary, the bigger problem was what to write. He had asked his elder brother who came for vacation from the city hostel.

"Write anything you feel, your joy, fears, anybody hurting you; but be careful don't put margins, it will eat space!"

Though he had his fancied own diary, he could hardly write much. He was afraid to write the fears, and to re-enact such scenes. After seeing the dead body in the well, near the school he had not slept properly for many a days.

At that times he wanted mother to be with him. But why should mother sleep in father's room only? It was a puzzle.

"Don't ask such questions" his elder sister told him seriously. "You will know when you are grown up?" Biggest mystery!

Many a times, including when he wanted have moustache, he had felt," When I will grow?"

He did grow, grow enough to even start writing something when a new teacher in English arrived. They were the days when mystery confounds, pains hurt, fears are imposing and joys turn scintillating. With his English now, diary was slowly becoming a pal. But 'diary' didn't fail him, it did wonders. Comforted in pain, filled hopes in despair and even laughed in joy. Also new teacher's one year, turned ON the flighty moods of the children. Poems of the gentle poets, with the teacher's explanations swayed their imagination. The copy of borrowed lines, got added to his words in the diary. The book, 'Anthology of poems', became too close. For the ones who dared to float, flair for words seeped in. In time, his diary became a detachable part of a pocket Thesaurus.

To sprout the real poet in him, needed an awakening. The real enchant days began, just as a rainbow in a summer.

It was school day function, where all winners in sports and cultural activities are honoured with prize. It was a proud moment to sit on a squeezed bench, sharing with winners. What suddenly pleased him was the girl pressing him, who was as beautiful as the champak flower on her plaits, in her dressed loose hairs. When her hands for congrats touched, it was his heart which she shook. It felt better than the prize he won- for poem writing. Soon the diary started smelling, with fresh champak flowers inside.

It was an age of undeveloped understands, curiosity to level of puzzle. It did stimulate him, unexplainable, even embarrassing to discuss with friends. Now the 'diary', though mute, could hold his thoughts and vibes.

But for outpouring his heart and for creativity, he needed solitude. The diary started visiting the banks of river, terrace and unsoiled benches of the park. Slowly, in a short time, diary captured his whimsical fancies as poems. Writing poems, became a hobby and even a past time.

Such delightful day's fleet fast. Though the heart was filled with colourful words to speak, the tongue held back. Earlier, many times he had wished to grow fast and shave like brother and go to college. Now, when the time arrived, it was a pinching hurt.

But the parting for the entry to college in a city, carried hopes. Surprisingly, the aroma didn't cease despite the absence of the flower! It surreptitiously followed him.

The pervading smell propelled many things. It was an inspiration to excel in academics, lift more weight in the gym, and bend in asana and even leap higher in games. They were the days of sprightly with a wonderful feel of future and focus to achieve them. The slender from a village, was turning buoyant youth. Even his diary became matured with a feel of float, sweet dreams and of prospect of hopes. The beaming face with moustache and the stimulations in the groin, heralded new dimension for his poems. Soon it became a beehive of poems, as sweet as honey.

The visits to native became purposeful, as the champak looked more beautiful and fragrant. When talking with her, the eyes shined, heart throbbed. What was disappointing, when all senses were fervent, his tongue failed to cooperate. It needed a year to stir the inertia and rigidity, to twist for the cause.

After a year when dared for the flow of words, the news of shatter- her engagement, ripped the fragile. It was hovering pathos imposing initially, then overwhelming him. The whole world seemed cruel. The bitterness pierced his heart.

The singing inner bird became mute. The exquisite aroma of champak drifted in the air, and even the sense of smell ceased. On an eventful day on the terrace of the hostel, his diary- also holding an 'Anthology of his poems', ceased its function, in tears. Once the blank unanswered sheets, filled with magical words now, spread into the gusty winds on a gloomy rainy day.

The seasons moved, carrying along with it all mortals.

In the final year at the college, the new room in third floor has large windows. The hall is spacious, illuminated by the bright sunshine of the season. The fresh breeze started opening his blocked nose, slowly, without explain. The sensitized nose could smell the circulating scent of a jasmine flower. In due times, jasmine became his favourite fragrance and the flower an adorable charm.

———————————————

14. PURITY

Siddhi was initially fascinated by the gymnasium, for abdomen packs. Like many among the youth.

After a few years, viewing his favourite body builder praising the ignored arts of India, also sought the 'flexibility of the body' and better utility of 'breathing air' for vitality; is learning them from the teachers in an Ashram in the city.

That was the motive, for 'Yogasana' and 'Pranayama'. After 4 to 5 years, he is experiencing the 'suppleness' and 'aerobic qualities'. Is even endorsing his instructor message, "It evolved, perfected over centuries".

Looking at the name plate on the Ashram, he always wonders for such a respect for the Seer, - 'Patanjali'! Many Wise men say, "He distilled all wisdom of techniques, ideas of earlier rishis into a feasible method for anyone, **in eight steps (levels)**".

But Siddhi cannot fathom the humanistic Seer, in bringing the 'spiritual aura', an esoteric wonder of a few elite, to common man's fold.

The Seer has organised the cardinal issues, in a simple frame work, retaining rigor. It is genius, beyond brilliance!

Siddhi had not imagined himself trying one of the levels, in a village branch Ashram, in a short time.

****

After finishing his regular sessions, is passing through the lecture hall, which he dared not to enter! On the black board it is written, by chalk piece. - "Lecture on the 5th level "..................."

He didn't bother for the word! One more from Sanskrit. He is always sceptic about people quoting Sanskrit words, to complicate simple issues.

To learn advanced techniques for "breathing' and 'bending, twice a week he visited here'.

Next week, he shared his curiosity with teacher, "Sir, what are the first four levels, which the Seer has defined."

"Do you adhere to ethics, morals in the society, with dignity? ". It is innocuous usual tone.

But the content hurt Siddhi sure. "Why not sir ", raised voice, unknowingly!

The teacher smiled; "then you have cleared the first 2 levels". He continued," it is conducting soundly, at personal and group levels."

Siddhi surely wished to continue. But the teacher smiled," Let us talk next week".

****

In the early morning, at the village ashram, Siddhi is feeling for a visit to the hillock nearby, which he knows now, in last two months. He is impressed by its serenity, ambience for solitude. Filling a few fruits in his bag hurried towards the hillock, for the morning practice.

The impressive hillock holds a scary respect. A folklore carries an ominous caution of wandering spirits in the nights; the fear is because of losing their eyesight, which can't bear the brightness of returning souls. It prevents habitation on the hillock.

> The souls of saints dwelled in the past,
> Commune to share their flow of thoughts;
> The blaze and beam of ethereal moulds,
> Dazzle the sneaks to hapless blinds!

It is a holy place, for the villagers. No one knows, when the open to winds temple was built, with the resident priest's absence. The Black stone infant- Krishna, on the altar receives the pooja on Sundays or on any festival days, as per a myth. There is a stone roof, with four pillars, to protect the idol and the devotees from the rains, when they visit. A basement is meant for sitting also.

Another interesting practice is, the cooking near the temple with materials from the homes. Eating is forbidden till rituals, prayers are completed. The imposition of fasting, with the chill of cold bath in the pond, is an endurance test. But the faith holds them steadfast.

In the end, when the least in variety food is eaten, it feels heavenly with the notions of surrender to supreme; it is sprinkles of holy scent.

For him, the pond on the mound is the thrill. It is filled by the trickles from unknown conduits, an elixir to drink. Some say, the spring is from the bottom sources also inside the pond, bringing the minerals. Taking bath before and after his routines is a rejuvenating experience. Sundays is his regular visits, unforgettable.

He is recollecting the teacher's words, eating the fruits.

****

"The 'Asanas' and the 'Pranayama' are the 3rd and 4th steps in the path of a yogi". It sounded sweet; a thrilling revelation! Has been practicing for several years now.

"Sir, am I eligible now to take on 5th level now?"

"Difficult to say. As per seer, you qualify. But 'sufficiency', I doubt?" There is hitch in his words.

"Sir, I want to know what is fifth, in simple terms".

"It is not simple as you think. The first four are 'physical'. This is about 'mind'."

The teacher sounded sober, "It's seeking inside".

The teacher's face turned kind, with some pride. Most including himself, dare such probe later in life. He saw an intent for honest sink, to seek depth. 'Is it not obligatory on me?' he thought.

"Hope it's not flash".

The nod of the pupil, meant all. The pat on his back, with words" can you have food with me, anyway it's Sunday- we can talk", reflected the teacher's consider.

"Tell me your honest feeling about 'Truth'?" the weighed words wanted authentic response.

"Sir, does 'Truth' really exist? I doubt because, if 'yes', why should it be so obscure. Why not we can feel it like the fruit juice, or the aroma of a flower at park?"

"Is it conjured story like a 'beautiful princess' at an island, after 7 oceans and 7 hills guarded by demons and beasts?"

Teacher is impressed.

"Nature is not partisan; Truth must be there everywhere, including our self. We don't feel it, because, it' is mind which should cognise the 'beautiful princess'. The devils, demons and beasts reside in, obstructing our mind"

"Precisely for that reason, the great Seer in his **first Sutra**, signifying the whole methods says, - **Yoga is removal of obstacles of the mind**, in one line". It is another revelation!

"Other Sutras detail how to do it, by methods, practices". He continued, with precision. Swami Vivekanda's 'Raja yoga', is half with replica of sutras; the other half is explanation for enlightening."

The Name sent a thrill in the speechless pupil.

"The first step 'inside the mind', is to know 'what mind is' and 'what it is not'. That is the step one, in the 5th stage."

"Let me hint the progressive steps, which the other stages deal"." Don't think on its enormity. It may confuse you." The teacher was cautious.

"Progressively, 'the controlling the mind' ensues."

"The impure mind, is like a veil of cataract, unable to see realities. Purification of mind will be the next issue."

"With the purity acquired, mind needs to focus like Laser, to steer through the barriers."

"With practice, motive and sustenance, the '**Dazzling Beautiful Crystal**' in its infinite mode will be felt, it seems. That is the bliss, 'Sath- Chith- Anand', a state of 'purity, compassion &, happiness'. - Which all of us aspire.

When Siddhi looked at the sculpture of the meditating Seer in the quadrangle, hither to unnoticed salient finer aspects dawned.

In the captivating stance, there is compassion, a glow of purity.

****

For siddhi, the experience in the open ambience is new; the singular exposure, rejuvenating.

He is feeling what the teacher had hinted:

"In Nature's enormity, your 'Asanas' become a feel of oneness with the animate, inanimate in the postures. You feel harmony in varied seasons by special breathing techniques; a unique feel of blend with the surroundings."

"Together they spur your internal energies."

****

"For the 'sufficiency' into 5th step, you need a different bent of mind. If you want I suggest a place, for 3 month's camp". Teacher's earnest suited the inclines of the interested; the curiosity is becoming an obsession.

The prime goal of this experiment is to realise that,' you are not your senses'. Senses are only collectors of information; your mind can observe it.

You try to spend your time close to Nature, with people surrounding. Importantly, you will learn to ponder the effects of sense organs on you. Later, that awareness may become a habit, even in the midst of routines, anywhere. The purpose of your sojourn is only these."

****

The sparse crowd is in the Sunday rituals, on an auspicious day.

A bright child of 8 to 10 years, is looking tired because of the imposed hunger, with beads of sweat on the hairs, forehead; he came to the hall, near its parents.

"When I can eat?

With mother's words, "in short time", is returning to resume the activities at the outdoor. Siddhi felt like handing over a fruit, from the bag. In the morning, one piece which is ripened and sounding the best seen in life, had made his tongue juicy like the mango.

When he picked up from the hand bag, it is the same one! There is a hesitancy to part that or one from others in the bag. Reconciling later, handed over the best one. In the child's eyes there is the same awe for the juicy mango, like what Siddhi had felt in the morn. Holding it like precious piece of trophy not to lose, went out.

When he glanced outside, after a few moments, he sees an old woman who asks alms on these occasions moving towards the boy and stretching her hand of begging. What he saw is unbelieving.

The child clutching the mango in hands voluntarily handed over it to the wrinkled wavering hands of old lady, spontaneously. There is no wavering like what he had a few minutes ago.

———————

For the first time in months' now, Siddhi is in deep thoughts, sitting in front of the idol alone, in the twilight of the evening. With the pleasant breeze and the orange light on his face, there is an overwhelming analysis, a stirring evaluation.

With the fascinating beautiful princess once reached, there is an allure to become a star in the sky, never to return to his islands back again. The pole star, Patanjali and many stars in the sky are guiding beacons to reach her. The single rowing boat can be steered through the turbulent sea, with the skills which can be learnt from other rowers. There are enough weapons left back by others to fight the demons and scary beasts.

May be, he may not be able reach the princess in one voyage? But when he is born again in some other island nearer to her, he can build another boat to resume the journey to reach her. The hope of becoming a 'star shining in the sky', can be enough impetus to drive him.

The other facet is glaring in the afternoon incident. When he looked at the idol, it is appearing like the child. 'Today's child', is a 'new discovery'. It is a spontaneous offer of sharing. Not the one like his; 'conceit', with drips of 'ego' soaked.

Closing his eyes, he focussed on the snap shot of the incident, before the boy is handing over the fruit to the old lady. There is a definite touch of 'concern', with 'purity', in its pristine beauty.

In the child of personification of 'purity', features of the face at the quadrangle is present.

Is it not worth to rediscover the 'child' in us, which shines with 'purity' and 'compassion', as a meaningful, realistic aspire?

It is tantalising moments of uncertainty, for his possible next move in life.

---

15. LIFE OF THE ARTISTS

As the joint secretary of the State administration, it is a pleasure to be a part of the official dinner, hosted by the Karnataka State, for the winners of the 'Strong Cultural activities', deep rooted in the region.

My incline to be active in sponsorship for the artists, began as the 'cultural activities leader' in the college, influenced more my being an artist of some exposure, and an innate passion.

Specifically, I am noting a few heartening changes happened over the three decades of my service. The sober decorum in the grand arena, with a glow in the faces of the numerous artists.' A satisfaction that the society has cognised their worth!' It is a definite indicate of the quality of life for many artists have now, affording more smiles.

Even I felt that the different schemes are helping the folk arts in the state, which was earlier often ignored!

I am recollecting the words of a great artist, which shaped my perceptions in the initial years of my administrative career.

"Artists are dreamers, floating in imaginations. Most don't have the skills to know how to walk in life to make a better living. When in peak, they fly with belief of permanency; but in distress the frail get shattered. Shear inability to handle, success and failures."

"Is it not the duty of the public to patronise them, when the artists uphold their culture, which public eulogise proudly?"

The simple man, though already a legend, had even pleaded.

"Please for heaven's sake don't do it. Am not discouraging a potential artist. But think of a rarest chance of possibility of improving artists' life, by state's patronage."

That had sealed by decision to hold on to the job.

****

A personal incidence proved one of solemn value in my life, with the thespian, a Dada phalke awardee from Karnataka in 1995, in a district of my first posting in IAS cadre; it was a matured advice which sustained my continuity, when a dilemma was imposing with adaptation problems, for an artist bent youth for admin job.

The idol was the special invitee from my side, representing district for the valedictory show of a famous drama troupe. It was befitting for the month's shows from the touring troupe, with some of them renowned as history, some in the twilight age now. For the ensuing

unofficial dinner at the district cultural hall, the artist bent Officer's overtures ensured goodwill from the rich in the city.

The chief guest who had gracefully accepted an invite to preside the last show, amidst his peak schedules, even volunteered to share moments of dinner with co-stars for personal touch. Only when the late night turned boisterous if not chaotic, my nerves tightened. The teetotaller artist, a keen observer, forced me to accompany him to outside to sit on a stone bench under a tree.

"I know what's in your mind. You are too young, an enthusiast, but with less exposure to the life of artists. They are here for the last one month for meagre returns, each day a struggle with hopes!"

I had confided almost a regret for arranging the dinner in the way it turned out. But the ripened did put a human touch for the episode.

"You have seen a few of them not touching much, while most crossed the limits. Do you know the common thing in all?"

I couldn't surmise the issue. "It is hunger and poverty for them and more so back in their homes for their wives and children. Some reacted with maturity not to get affected by a day's flourish. But the most, preferred to drown their helpless anguish in the other way."

"They forget it only when they are on the stage, or otherwise in sleeps of exhaust. It haunts them always"

When new awareness dawned, I tried to discuss my predicament of continuing my job, or seeking to become an artist. He became very cautious and pleaded even!

"Please for heaven's sake don't do it. Am not discouraging a potential artist. But think of a rarest chance of possibility of improving artists' life, by state's patronage."

"That can prove a yeomen service to artists' fraternity". "Please do this without wavering. Always remember my words without getting carried away in your status improvements, later."

When I was on the bed in the early morning after that night, the emphasis had reminded me an incident already experienced, while I invited an artist of exception, which had slipped my mind. I was secretary for the cultural group in the college, inviting a National award winner for his role as poor Dalit father. A memorable natural performance.

****

Some of us from the college who finally could locate his house in an impoverished area, had seen many children playing outside, some with unusual clothes of shorts. For the wife it was embarrassing to see unexpected guests visiting, being not prepared. Sensing it my friend told," Just a few minutes back we had coffee in the corner hotel"

The artist in his usual bristles of beard, uncombed hair with deep penetrating eyes looked more like the hero of the movie, which had gained him national level acceptance. When asked about the secret of lively performance, in the path breaking poignant role, his reaction in deep voice, was curious.

"I didn't act, it was a chance to be in natural reality!" Thanking us gladly he accepted the invite and after half an hour accompanied us up to the city bus stand. Sensing my role as the organiser who takes decision, gracefully managed to have a chat with me, personally.

"Son, I have a small request. Please don't honour me with Shawls. All I received in recent months are used for children clothes, bed sheets, bed spreads and curtains. Many I sold them back to shops at half the price. If it is possible, give it in cash to be useful for children's school fees."

Sensing things, while parting I gave him sizable money in the guise to cover for his trips to our town. While he gladly accepted it, I couldn't avoid noticing his glistened eyes.

Now, in the early morning tosses on the bed I realize the shade of drops in his eyes is not for the self-pity of poverty, but for the dent on his self-respect!

16.   IMPRACTICAL

Nalini's wink, with a mischievous smile said it all. Perhaps that is her last but one level, to put things plain.

Nagesh, is not dumb; both know it. Her basic question is why? The young looking divorcee in mid-thirties and her younger brother's friend are strolling on the roads on a late evening in New York's downtown in a weekend.

To meet sometimes his close friend, though a little senior in the college is hearty for him. Amidst the hectic schedules of masters' at Syracuse, a nearby university, and because of loneliness in the campus, the visits can be simply invigorating.

Their families know one another from a long time at Bangalore. Today is a rare, to meet some other members who have gathered for a family occasion; from all over the regions.

In his beginning of college days, the ever green event is the Nalini's marriage, almost a decade back. Whenever he crossed the marriage hall in Bangalore, with festoons of Mango leaves or decorative lamps, he remembered, '35 dishes of Kerala marriage', sounding more like his favourite movie, '36th chamber of Shaolin'. Her marriage with an NRI, became a passport for her brother's entry to USA.

"What is your plan for Christmas?" It had started it all. Before he could come out of confusion, she has suggested. "Why not we go to Niagara?" Even in her younger days, she was known for plain openness. But now it is presumptions laced in imagines!

His startled response, "With river as ice", is more of a reason to avoid by the fidgety!

"Why visit to falls, the rooms are cosy, the hot swimming pools and a week together can be just wonderful in privacy!" It is the final open- invite offer from her; the best she could put it across, to the embarrassed conservative! She knew he is alone, almost 2 years, in final stages of his master's to return to join his family and wife back in India.

He is wondering and couldn't hide the surprise, "How much you changed in a decade"!

But she is matured to understand his predicament.

Finally, in sober voice said, "Nagesh, this is most unusual from my side also. I am lonely now for a few years. It is painful in plenty here. This is confused phase in my life. I can share, I thought with someone known. It is not only the stretches in bed I need, but some soothe I am longing; though the former, hope can be exciting with you." She is in her enigmatic smile again.

She continued driven by her hurts in life," I don't want to return to India, at least immediately, with a feel of void. Need to achieve something in life; then can be shift and new begin"

Probing her withered face now, could feel the pangs in loneliness which he is tuned to himself. He felt her dilemmas, which haunt most in this otherwise prosperous country; for immigrants could be more painful away from their soil,

"I am sorry."

Her last words is touching," Life taught an innocent girl from India to turn 'practical' now; just a matter to survive mentally".

But he is impractical enough not to become sentimental!

"I appreciate your attitude; your wife is lucky", is her last words in the late evening. In the glistened eyes there is no trace of guilt though. They entered to the big family and friends' inside the house.

****

In the Christmas holidays' brooding, the word, 'practical', reverberated. Because that word, has a lot of association in his life!

Father was a practical, as a police inspector to amass a mini fortune, to own a decent house in the centre of city and a few acres of fertile agriculture lands, nearby. He could make his first son, a lawyer and marry off his two daughters to decent families. For the last son, sensing his academic abilities had catered enough for his engineering studies.

The only wrong thing in father's life was indulgence in drinks and the habits, which perhaps he had rationalised, as practical, to end prematurely. It was just before Nagesh could join Engineering.

Nagesh had liked his eldest sibling with an age difference of more than 15 years, in lawyer' robe. He turned real professional with a rare commitment to become famous; so famous, an influential powerful politician gave his daughter to inspector's first son. Everything was fine till the sister in law was declared barren and in a few years her depressions triggered uncontrollable, Asthma.

That was a beginning phase for the brother, who slowly became a practical more like his father! Why a lawyer didn't go for second marriage or divorce, is speculative for Nagesh? 'Powerful father in law or a negative mark in the society; or even the disapproval of mother, who is still owning all father earned?'

Before leaving the country had met his professor, now the vice chancellor, a Gandhian who is wedded to dreams from younger days; remained same for life. Had survived on self-prepared village dish for two to three years for a doctorate here.

He had touched the word 'Practical'. "Its deception to cover weakness. Like the politicians telling,' there is no friends or foes in politics'." Looking at the photo on the wall, "Only some strong purpose in life can keep away such tempts"

The one in his life, his mother, definitely impractical whence most sound 'practical' as 'a virtue' for selfishness.

Perhaps he is more like her. Her contention is clear." You don't go after things. If you deserve, they will come to you", a fair advice to reinforce his beliefs.

Even she had surprised him, when she made him to marry the smart girl in the neighbourhood, who visited regularly to talk to his ailing sister in law and old mother. She had declared at that time, 'you need a smart wife in your life to balance'. Not that he was not inclined for the offer, though.

The things had happened fast. His job in MNC, subsequent alliance with known family. The wife only had enthused him with the notions of higher studies for prosperity in the long term. It was a 'smart move', nothing wrong in aspiring.

"We can move to States. When you study there, you keep an eye on that. That will change our future".

"But we are just married for a year now, and had planned for a child in the next year."

"Sometimes a small sacrifice can make big difference in life; I can go through things." It was an unexpected resolve hinting strong mind!

"But what about finances, it is huge". That was when the wife impressed by her entrepreneurship, to make the others and brother to agree to sell a few acres of land in the village. Though Brother was clear to make the point "It is from Nagesh's share", when mother signed the papers.

Nagesh is appreciating everything that happened when the months moved, to come to the final ones.

****

When the flight arrived in the early morning at Bangalore, the big suit cases is his waiting worry. His taxi could breeze through the vacant roads, to his house in the very early morn, with fresh smell of flower city. With the driver helping to bring the luggage, he pressed the bell.

When the lights switched ON, one by one and door opened it is a pleasant surprise for the wife. For him equally surprising is the more beautiful wife, a little plump with a red shine in her cheeks. When he moved to meet mother," She is coming in the morning with your sister. Last one week she is there, for Chotu's thread ceremony. Your flight we thought will reach tomorrow afternoon?"

"In the last moment I could change it". In the intent to meet the dear ones early, a few hours sound precious!

When the wife went to kitchen to make husband's favourite Coorg coffee, he decided to talk with the brother with presents of the scotch brand. Opening the tight door, he saw his brother in inebriated condition murmuring his dreams, even unable to sit up. Leaving the bottles, came back to hall, closing the door.

While drinking his favourite elixir which he missed for a long time, peeped into sister in law and wife's common room.

"She has severe bouts now a days. Only after one in the early morning, she gets sleep. That too with a sleeping pill, which I give."

"He felt sorry for his wife, who is going through all this services".

She asked him to take bath in their room and she went for hers in the sister in laws common room now.

****

When he is pressing the mother's legs gently in the sister's house, talking to her for half an hour, there is no puzzle now in his face; a puzzle like the one which was on his happy wife's face, a few hours earlier; it was when he asked for the brother's bike keys, even without taking bath.

Now he is recollecting the offers at States. The face of Nalini with a rare glow due to absence of pretentions haunted.

The initial worried face before he could spend moments with mother has changed to one of resolve; the change inexplicably happened, in the vicinity of mother, when he decided to continue what he is!

His senses are practical still; to hear the brother's murmurs, to smell the faint aroma in the hall when he entered and to see the first light switching ON, when he pressed the calling bell!

---

17. PAINTING

[A part of this story, 'Nangeli', is in the proposed making of a movie, with Angelina Julie, under the direction of renowned Dr. Raja Nair.' Inspired by 'a real story' narrated by a friend from Kerala]

It is a serious bother for Sheshu. His 'conscious efforts' is resulting in less of 'creativity.'

The reputed artist of painting, needed a memorable one for his exhibition in a gallery. It is annoying, as he is in need of the best piece for his self-satisfaction; an endurable one to become 'a stamp of his name'.

He is even doubting the absence of 'sparks', the moments when the 'inward eye', flashes different meanings in ordinary things. A voice of 'instinct' had always prodded him, when the creative moods eluded. It hinted to free the mind, by letting it go.

The invitation to attend an 'international culture program' organised by Kerala state, did the trick! The visit to the places of the state of 'pristine beauty', with a few co-artists and a meet with international artists can be fascinating! The yearnings slipped out of his mind.

****

131

He became a child in its variety and grandness. Green everywhere, with people cordial and simple; not many can match the state.

The plantations of Tea, Coffee, Pepper and Cardamom; The natural water reservoirs, the man made back water reservoirs, the plain and cascading waterfalls; the trekking in winding slope hills, cascade walks, stay at log houses; the fresh mountain air, wildlife and bird sanctuaries, enchanting retreats; ever green forests, misty mountains; the sea beaches and boating to nearby islands – a heaven on earth!

****

The latest buzzing news is the treasure of the temple at Thiruvananthapuram. Remembered the excerpts from, News Asia publication,

"The forgotten and cursed 20 billion treasure trove is unearthed beneath an Indian temple".

This news is wild, creating an unheard curiosity in the country. The suggested antique value is a tenfold hike. The trust is the richest in India, may be second only to Vatican. More people sought to know the history of the treasure, because of the news.

The surprise starts in the mid-18th century, when the local royal family took a stunning decision, to dedicate themselves as servants of God, 'Dasas'; a dramatic one in the annals of world history. But the implications are many.

One is, the excess in their fortunes to be merged with that of temple to create a new build. The second is more significant to dedicate it to a temple 'Trust." To locate the treasure physically under the temple in cellars, is the third.

Why the mighty who had won many a wars decided, is speculative? Is it act of a repentance for the bloodshed experienced or some other?

"Did the royals reduce the tax burden on the people?" it confused the guide!

"As far as I know, it was not sir. But, they did divert the treasure during natural calamities, once in a few decades", was tricky!

****

The visit to the temple inside, is a rare experience; the grandeur is stunning!

The principal Deity is 'Vishnu', enshrined in the posture of 'Yogic sleep', on the giant serpent' Adishesha'. The reclining on the mighty five hooded serpent with three coils, is majestic. From the naval of the lord, a lotus stem emerges to house 'the god of creation', in a lotus flower. Under the stretched right hand, 'the god of destroy', Shiva is placed, all in shining gold.

It is truly symbolic of the presumed 'Nature', in essence. The five hoods, are the sentinels, earth, sky, fire, air and water. The three coils reflects the moulds of individuals as three 'Gunas', which signify the 'attitudes' transitorily changing in humans. The three deities of birth, sustain and death, remind the cycle of life.

The lord in the sleeping posture with glitters of gold covers and diamond studded crown, is a mix of awe and devotional respect for the believers, an amazing experience for any visitor. Its spell lasts for some times.

But, when he closed his eyes and meditated, a strange feel ensued. How magnificent it would have been as a sculpture in single black stone when it was made; a symbol in Nature's bosom in an open arena! Without the glitters.

The 18 feet mural behind the sanctum, the virtual replica, is a wonder for the artists.

****

In the festival, the programs are interesting. One from the local group, an evening short musical is impressive.

The whitebeard man, with a dignified grace is holding the mike on the stage. Behind him in a row, his troupe of youngsters in white traditional cotton saris and white Dhotis are standing. He is also in a white dhoti, along with a cotton hand bag on his shoulders.

"Ladies and Gentleman,

It is a great privilege for my team to be here in this "International Cultural meet', organised in Kerala. We present an adapted version of our popular, musical drama with commentaries; though truncated, efforts are made to retain the original rigor and the vigour. With no actors on the stage, the background painted screens hint at the locale and the actors. The commentary with the singing chorus and the music, does the rest.

Our effort is to recall a sacrifice in its entirety, with powerful visuals to the sensitive. Hence our request, for the children are not be part of this visuals. We seek the mature audience to receive with a feel of the context; and our intent is to avoid such gory, manmade situations in future.

This valiant story of this land, dates back by 200 years. 'Nangeli' the icon, is famed to be one of the first feminists in the history in the world. Her stirring saga has inspired and is inspiring thousands to date, for her sacrifice for a cause. The significance of the episode lies in its becoming the harbinger of social traumas for ensuing decades, for the state and even for neighbours.

It was the time when the rulers turned greedy, sadists and for filling coffers, imposed one of 5 queerest taxes in the world, till now. With a covert intent to sustain the luxury life for a few, the laws were framed to deprive the prosperity for the large populace.

This story is of a lady, who defied one of the laws valiantly, finally succumbing, but shaking the roots of the whole system.

Her courage is unparalleled, the conviction peerless and the determination unique.

Her end melts us for a few drops of tears. It prods to be vigilant for the possible veiled threats, in guise. Her story instigates to voice and struggle for any injustice."

In the first scene, the background is a screen indicating 'the green paddy field, with coconut trees' behind. A few girls bending, are in the act of cutting the paddy.

Commentary:

Our Nangeli, the beautiful Nangeli, is in the chorus of a folk song. Swaying the head to the rhythm, the belle is sharing her joy of mirth with others.

"We are the butterflies floating in the air,
Upping our feelers looking everywhere;
We drink, the flowers, for its sweet honey,
Honey, oh! Relish we that lovely honey."

These sprites filling the fields with their magical presence, are in the green age looking for the nectar of life, seeking a companion.

The screen changes to a marriage view with relatives and friends, in laughing mood. The groom Kandappan, and our lady, are stretching hands to shake. They also seek an approval for their betrothal, from others.

Commentary:

Nangeli, did get the companion, with a pledge to be partners during in- life and even in- death. Together they wanted to share the happiness and sorrows, supporting each other.

"The blooming bride stretched her hand,
Looking for a promise to hold till end;
The beaming groom, seized the soft hand,
Vouching a trust sealed an eternal bind"

The seeking- 'for a trust in all the days of life', was pledged. Only the time will judge whether 'steps in concur', will materialise or not?

Nangeli, our pretty Nangeli, subsumed into the wedlock, with a hope and aspire to lead a beautiful life.

The years rolled and they needed a different dimension for more meaning. That was when the delicate Nangeli, presented her husband a child: 'a giggling tot'. Both hoped the new arrival will ease their strife, to endure.

The stage was dark without light. But in a voice of lament, the commentary continued.

Commentary:

Strife, yes. It was unbearable strangles imposed by the 'wild bee', ruling the kingdom, in terms of taxes.

Man left to himself was happy with what Nature gave. Found the mates, rejoiced with the Nature's tunes in her offers, and could bear even its fury.

In the end man departed, leaving his trail of presence; decayed to be consumed with the soil, water, fire, sky and the air; but with, a glad of content and a feel of full.

But to make society organised, the rulers sprouted. Invariably turned greedy, cruel; more so for the vulnerable ones.

The scene is Nangeli sitting in the house, with baby on her lap in of ponder.

Commentary:

The hurts of poverty is painful, painful not only because it hurts one; more because of seeing others whom one cares, suffer. Can there not be any reprieve for these, targeting the few? Is there a miracle to bring our joys, which we need and deserve?

"The pangs of strife withered the soft,
More with the stings of wild bee's bite;
The despair gloomy prayed at the sky,
With a fond hope for the restore of joy."

Nangeli, the poor Nangeli, from a floating butterfly slid unto one of helpless prey.

It was darkness again, with no light on the stage, even in the hall; to signify the gloom to follow. The stage became darker, with a long sober commentary.

Commentary:

Nangeli, the legend Nangeli, is not hailed for her beauty and grace, nor even for her feel of integrity to the family. Many flowers bloom in this land and perish. In the imposing glooms others only lament, but endure somehow!

But here is the singular incidence, whence one fought back; in the process etched her name in history. Why this story is cherished even now, is the act on that day.

One of the 5 queerest taxes in the history of society is - 'tax on breast covering, for a specific community'. We loathe it, but that was the pervert the rulers stooped; a token of methods to keep some lower the ground and **to add another coin to their coffers.**

———————

The lights switched ON including the one on the stage. The scene had a lighted lamp, placed on a banana leaf, a symbol of the land, for festive days.

Commentary:

Defiant Nangeli, covered her bosom. It became an act of challenge to the authorities. The vigilant stooges of the king with power bestowed, swooped her home with demand of 'the queer tax". She went inside the room with a resolve, for the last feed to the child.

"Sweet is the joy of the suckling feed,
Nature's boon for mother's pride;

Knowing it's the end, the breasts swelled,
Flowing the nectar in a copious flood.

She came back? Sure. With the tax, to be placed on the fresh banana leaf. Holding the symbolic tax in her hands, she placed it on the leaf.

In a dramatic sway of seconds, light switched off for a pause, turns the stage to a diffused red light, with scene changed. It's the same banana leave, but with the tax beside Nangeli, stretching on the leaf and swooning.

The commentator's voice is full of pathos, with pity. The low background music, in violin, reflected his voice.

Commentary:

Nangeli, did give the tax, on the banana leave. It's her **sheared breast.**

In a voice of rage she shouted to the taxman to take it to the king.

"Command I thee, to take my offer,
Carry it to the king to fill his coffer;

The valiant Nangeli, by the time her husband came back, is no more, stretching on the banana leaf. The act of Kandappan, her husband by itself is remarkable, of jumping into the pyre to join her.

"He held his promise to hold till the end,
Proved his vouch for the eternal bind;
Both melted in their fury of despair,
Sliding unto glory on the burning pyre.
Alas, why?
Why did they forget their piece of heart?
To create an orphan in their rash act?

[The commentator's voice changed to one of rage and fury]

The land wept for the news. But it triggered massive retaliation. The dormant disgust on themselves came out of the masked veil. Before the sparks in pyre cooled, the collective anguish consumed many.

"The stirring story kindled the ire,
Spreading the land, like a wild fire:"

The obdurate rulers then proved shrewd; by hasten repealed the law.

The sacrifice of Nangeli, did not go in vain and later, changed the course of history.

****

The silence in the audience for a long time, signified its impact; the visuals with the musicals made a different dent.

The later in the sessions of different days, the ballet from Russia, swayed the audience to different world with spectacular 'Swan swings'. The traditional 'Jazz' from America, swung the time back by a few decades. The enactment of a drama from the English troupe, reminded the genius of 'Bernard Shaw'. The acrobatic show from the Chinese artists is spell binding. The melodies in instruments from the Japanese, soul stirring, reflected the perfection seeking in natural environs, their 'Zen' way.

****

In the refreshing return of the team, each carried own memorable experiences from the abundant variety. Sheshu had two options for his subject now.

It's an evening with a few friends of the same team, including the new artist, a dancer of repute for a simple dinner and plenty of drinks, in Sheshu's home. For the new friend, the small studio is interesting, with the copy of a painting 'sunflower' of Vincent Van Gog, the Dutch artist who changed the perception in painting.

For Sheshu," He is my Guru in absence, changing my life to what I am. Stirs me and motivates, even now".

Under the painting of a 'simplistic beauty', a placard has the words of the icon painter-

"I dream of painting and then I paint my dream".

For the new friend, the canvas being ready for a new one 'with dust accumulated', is puzzling!

Sheshu in his own eloquence is analysing, "Painting is synthesis of experiences"; the quote is another inquisitive set of words for the new acquainted! The party in the leisure for the artists' inclines, lasted long into the late night.

The next day, Sheshu woke up late in the morning, that too on the floor of his studio. It is a shocker of experiences for him, first time in decades of profession! In stunning silence looked at the canvas!

The finer aspects are depicted, with subconscious imprints in dazzling colours. The moods portrayed, even baffled its own creator! It is a synthesis of the two impressions, but in poignancy!

Sheshu could fathom the depth in Vincent's words, now.

---

18. RELIGIOUS

In the solemn moments of life swayed by gloom, analysis and logic hide by retreat, words cease, and the stark reality bares one.

Only the subconscious belief deep rooted, comes to the fore.

I looked at the placard on my table, which is always dearer to me, for the last one and half decades. The casing has improved as the tables changed, to bigger one in a cosy cabin over the years. But the same script retained is unique.

God give me:
> The courage to change the things which I can,
> The serenity to accept the ones which I cannot,
> And the wisdom to know the difference.

-- Anonymous.

That memorable day signified a lesson; the day when my assumed affinity to **words** proved hollow, skin deep; a stamp for 'intellectual fascination!' For my recovery it has taken days, after an eventful day; first time to sleep with a pill, for days.

But it was also the day when, the most affected family in distress conducted in a remarkable way. The episode made me **honest** to accept my limitation to fathom, the essence of courage, serenity or wisdom!

****

I am with my friend in the beginning of forties who is big hearted, literally with one in the ICU. Soon, it is a sensitive time for me to come out to convey the news, which we had feared most.

His father, wife and sisters on the benches in dreary state are hoping for a miracle. The tears has ceased in the red swollen eyes. The two young children in jittery strolls in the hall meant much to me. Other friends are standing in the periphery of the sitting, in helpless confusion.

Slowly dragging my feet moved to the septuagenarian father. The squeeze of hand with the fragile and my head nod, conveyed eventuality. It was irrepressible tears in all, though is a restrained reaction in the hall. The only faint sounds ruffling the hall is the close knit family hugging one others, murmuring in grief!

The father whispered to me," God should have taken me, how can I bear this?"

The wife's dazed eyes looked nowhere, hugging the two sons. I went to her and stood sometime in silence to remind the decision taken a few days back. My friend had signed with wife's concur for the donation of any part, if he ends in demise. He had convinced his wife, "This is best I can offer to God".

Other friends arranged for the family to return home, with some of us waiting for formalities and completion of donation.

****

For the flow of people, friends and relatives of the popular family, while paying last rites in the home, it is a strange experience. No overtures or rapturous outbursts.

The father in lotus posture, sitting straight as a tree, is a statue with equanimity lit on his face. His half open eyes focussing on the tip of the nose, and the moving lower lip suggests deep meditation. In front of the head of family, is the son's body with spread of flowers.

The sandalwood fragrance and the flames of the oil lit lamps in the pooja room suggests the group prayer of the family earlier. Most of the twenty plus in the close knit other than jittery children, are resting their back on walls near the edges of floors. The ones with closed eyes, had deep breaths in silence. The old man's influence has percolated to all. The witness for the proceeds is the photo of the seer, Sri Raghavendra Swamy, in a big frame on the wall above the tormented.

In the poignant moments of their life time, an amazing sense of moderation is visible. In the gloomy envelope there is collective feel of total surrender. That day, recollecting the prayer of my friend, I felt,

'The power of sincere belief in religion.'

Om,
  From Delusions lead me to Truth,
  From Darkness lead me to Light,
  From Death lead me to Eternity.

Om, Peace, Peace, Peace. Brihad Aranyaka Upanishad.

---

19. TUTOR

I felt embarrassed for my unusual wry smile, though luckily was sure no one will be observing in the twilight evening.

The same place sitting now, was witness for the start of the flow of events, absorbing two years; most meaningful in recent decades of my life. But my earlier enthusiasm, now sounded a deception. The vagaries of mind, volatile perceptions possible even amused me. Those refreshing years had crystallised with my old friend's words!

"It will be a noble cause, if you can do it".

I was sitting on the stone after decades, looking at the once river bed of 'North Pennar'; an undercurrent river. The encroachments and the depletion of sand, did not suggest the younger day's scene. With a local friend, I had shared the other concern of bigger gravity, an hour back.

'The district turning barren in education, sliding to 28th place in the state, from the earlier, one in top few!' My father, always a hopeful soul, who lived here for sixty years laments, "Still there is 3 to 4 places to reach bottom!" It echoed the mood of the most, a sign of helpless distress!

From the early evening I am observing the groups of some students, luckily now with sandals and most in full pants, returning to their villages from the town. The wind in the outskirts is comfortable, than inside the haphazardly mushroomed houses in the town.

My 'possible idea' to prepare some poor bright children for engineering entrance to the state colleges, enthused my old friend. There was a rare glow in his face. He became emotional,

"Such a thing never happened here. It will be 'oasis in desert'!"

I could feel his excitement. In my occasional visits of once in a few months for a couple of days, the local realities had not dawned. Even if I had noticed, perhaps I would have reacted like others. 'The equality of opportunities, is a myth and mirage!'

Though the brightest in the school class, he became a help boy in the municipal office, a post offered when his father died young. Now a clerk, is living frugally for decades. He has sent his two sons to Tumkur for studies, under the Matt. A glimmer of hope.

"My only dream in life is to make them, what they deserve",

There was a flash in his tired eyes, which covered a sense of resign, accepted long back.
But my genuine doubt to him was, "can it make a difference here?"

He was emphatic, hardened by his own life. "If you can change the lives of even five, is it not worth?"

With a possibility that my notions can be a fleeting wish, philosophically ended,

"May be a drop in ocean, but is not the ocean less if the drop if not filled?"

It did stir my psyche.

'The idea' is not a sudden one, like a spring rush. A convergence of a few factors. Some are motives imprinted in my mind. The best was the great 'Kumar' of Bihar, proving the potentials of thirty down trodden kids for IITs. Every year. Listening and meeting him, can infect his conviction.

Second is the live example in Rajaiah, my senior in my school days. A lifelong friend and my idol. Son of a sheep herdsman with a small dry land, to top in the pre university from the college here and IIT later, to be a Director of Software giant, at Bangalore now.

"Why not some other gems from the same mine!"

The third is purely personal. My daughter scaling high in such tests, under my guidance. The thought made me to sit erect, with more air filling the lungs. For a Master graduate in physics, working in the sick public sector, who is on less paid salaries for fifteen years, it was a life time pride! Her job in an MNC, hastened my Voluntary

Retirement Scheme; a break from vicious circuit of no comebacks.

But shortly, an unexpected turn ensued. A minor head injury for the unmarried brother, an employee of rural bank here, sounded a bugle from the once in a week visiting Neuro physician. "Possibility of drain in chemicals, if unattended. Medicines and rest for two years, at least."

The presumed indifferent unmarried brother, looked fragile, pitiable. Now, I realised his tending services to old father, including cleaning of drips of urine in the hall, the occasional excreta on the night beds; my blissfully ignored responsibility. The sight of fiercely independent father who taught till 80 years, with the brother's plight stirred the conscious.

The best time in the town was a visit to my college, on an afternoon. The unexpected flourish is one more affinity of Rajaiah with the college. University Grants Commission's patronage is a source of funds, great salaries for the disbelieving staff.

The same board, looking repainted now, invited in the front.

"Savidyaya Vimuktaye, meaning, '**Education is true liberty**'. I felt now, 'how true'. The place moulded hundreds to become graduates. More so for scores of girls, who otherwise couldn't have even dreamt! Like my elder sister, a house wife who kindled skills for her children.

The other new boards read the earlier words of wisdom. Surely difficult to replicate!

'**A home that has a library, has soul in it**'- Plato's gentle fond wish, led to a spacious, less utilised library. Glancing the referred pages was nostalgic. The lines underlined dodging the Librarian's vigil, brought a smile.

In the entrance of the labs, '**No teachings here, but environ for self- learnings**', the words of Einstein, echoed the first principal's aspires; a motivating exacting soul, for the staff to find their own peaks.

The modern Gym, motivating packs for the youth, has replaced the rural, traditional wrestlers den of sand grounds, a few swirling sticks and iron weights; I remembered the sand brought by us from the river bed; more involved activity than completing the home works.

I wondered though such possibilities of packs for the less protein eating children. But it highlighted the same motto, '**A sound body is foundation for divine temple**".

But missing the best one, did hurt. "**Our true goal – Education with culture, character**".

The one acre horticulture land on the banks of river bed, inside the edge of college premises, had signified,' moral and cultural activities'; Music, dances, yogasanas amidst greenery. The place, where we were exposed to Vedas, philosophers, including western.

Now it has the extensions for Arts College, the big cycle stands and the new basketball asphalt ground with fibre transparent boards. For many years, to the demand of a small cycle stand, the principal looking at the shades of green trees had brushed it smilingly, postponing for paucity of funds.

"Cycles have own stands anyway?"

The asphalt court, a symbol of the college tradition thrilled me, a player in the '**barefoot team**'; the same phrase was the teasing words of echo in the finals at the Kanteerava Stadium finals at Bangalore.

The evening finals was everything for the new coach, a local state player, an alumnus from the YMCA. For the uncouth players it was a pleasant disbelief in the run. It became a horror, to play the finals on the first asphalt court with fibre boards, not exposed.

In dreams of basking in glory, the coach felt no option. To induce higher jumps in the best shooter to ward off tall defenders, he fed his elixir, like during his crucial moments of events. With the last evening snacks before the match, sips of rum was the antidote; even to decrease anxiety.

The first minutes in the night match was mixed, with defenders doing well, but the best shooter in disarray to coach's dismay. When the game appeared slipping, took a long rest call. Unable to explain, I had confessed. "Am seeing two rings, though jumping higher!" My lament continued,

"Tried with both the rings".

He smilingly encouraged," Don't shoot at any ring, aim open space in between. That was my own strategy" He was somehow confident of the team!

It was a decisive win, for three of us to become coveted 'State junior players'. More importantly a delight to wear,' the first canvas sports shoes'.

The other day, entering the barber shop was unavoidable.

The valve radio replaced by the mp3 set is running the choice songs. The possible choice has made the best tunes less melodious. The annoyance when a teenage changed his required style to a different one in the middle, contrasted my rushing back for more reduce in bushy hairs; the parents dictate. It had resulted in focussed trimming.

I could avoid the next tailor shop, now, "Bombay tailors". The old tailor stitched longer half pants annoying the children; but he had to honour the paying parents. " They grow faster". He had readymade matching square patches for the torn ones; the overactive children brushed their bottom on soiled grounds and the stone floors of schools.

The third shop surprised with the friend, now the richest in the town. He took me to the best treat of snacks in the only good hotel. To my query, he answered,

"They were in the best residential schools and now are in the college wings". My eyebrows didn't hide.

"That is how it is. Rich send to residential, the middle class find sudden affection to relatives in bigger towns and cities. The long term loans by them is rewarding me". The enterprising, winked;

"Anyway, where are the teachers like your father?" He did hint on the other aspect.

"Poor just go through life. Most, not even aware why they are poor!"

The other decisive moments was at the college, on a pleasant morning. My back bent now, became straight; like the earlier athletic lad had. It was after humming the old college prayer, in chorus with more voices, now.

The benevolent father, Lead us to truth holding our hands:

> Spur us to glow to dispel the darkness,
> Like the wick burning the oil and itself;
> Cheer us to spread the divine scents,
> Like the wild fragrant flowers in the woods.

The generous kind, Lead us to truth holding our hands:

> The guiding star in the turbulent seas,
> Propel us to endure the testing times;
> Fill us the content to feel the full,
> As the mother earth in her bounty feed.

The compassionate soul, Lead us to truth holding our hands.

The data to find the addresses and the marks, of the brightest poor in the first year of course, led to search for better ones in the other three nearby colleges. The teaching for the entrance is ideal in the second year of the course.

There was no dearth of talent. More surprise was the reaction from the beedis smoking, tobacco chewing parents. The bait of the biscuits, bananas with Badam milk for children in the evenings, was a more surprise than free tuition. The demand for a better space for study in the house, is the grouse, who don't even see their ward's marks sheets!

The things are in place within a month. Physics and Maths for 2 hours a day, with mock tests on Sundays. The proud big black board of father proved useful. The big hall in the house needed clearing everything and a few new tube lights. The twenty children learnt by sitting on the mats; most resting the back on the periphery of walls.

Then I remembered the card in my old leather purse for the need of ten sets of books, each to be shared by two. Holding the card I recollected;

Rajaiah, had not forgotten the smell of his soil and a few dispersed seeds from his village. My wife's only reason to be in his daughter's wedding was possible help for her two children. Like the caterpillar becoming a butterfly, the nature holds many riddles including women! My words," True warmth doesn't need frequent meets or proof, it's just trust", had failed to convince her.

Introducing me to his wife," Another bright from village college," had hurriedly thrust his card into my white shirt pocket, priding reading glasses and a pen. His affectionate words, "Any time you call; it is not disturbance', meant what he is. My wife's response," I believe what you said", sufficed the magnetic appeal of the genuine.

———————

In a short time miracles happened.

The books for the children is from the legend. In an unexpected visit on a Sunday, the two members of a foundation felt a cause to support and even had a professional advice.

"Why not 'house' the needy children during the exam months. We will bear the food cost."

A chemistry professional who visits his farm of vegetables and flowers was ready to spend a couple of hours on Sundays, for a fees and diesel charges for his car. Even brother started involving in tests and valuations, apart from preparing Badam milk in the evenings.

Is it a fable, I wondered! Dr. Abdul Kalaam's words," Dream is the need", seemed possible. In deep slumber even had a wild one. To create the 'rainbow troopers', of Andrea Hirata, every year.

Two things I learnt from the chemistry professional. The skills to make children learn themselves and unimagined monetary value for the tutors in the city!

We entered the compound gate into Rajaiah's spacious house at JPNagar, with our faces dull, wilted stems in these summer days. It is a heartfelt concern for the lifelong admirers, for his crippling health. To see the amputee of legs, stirred the ones surrounding him, gently holding his hands. Though the bright eyes retained the glow, the layer of drops masked it. Soon from his feeble voice we deciphered that it is not because of self-pity, but for not reaching his goals. We didn't want to tire him by his talks.

The last time I had talked with him was for thanking him for the books donated and for sending the foundation people. Before coming, I was planning to brief him about a letter.

"Though you have quoted as personal problems, we note with regret your untimely stoppage of illustrious work you are carrying on for two years. We are surprised to see your decision, even shocked. You are an example we quote. Any day you resume, hope you will, we extend our hands".

Even I wanted share with him, the complete absence of acknowledge to my sacrifice for two years. 'The town lacked collective soul', was my anguish. Now, I felt not to disturb.

But the last words of Rajaiah is stunning!

"Naga, you proved wiser than me. I wanted to do it, after becoming CEO. Thought myself eternal". His spirit recovered immediately. "I will come, teach on wheel chairs", is his resolve.

———————

The hall in the house at the town renamed as 'Paramahamsa nilaya', after the silence for a year is echoing.

"Physics is, learning about Nature and Mathematics is, its language"

The photo-frame above the black board, enclosing the smiling face of Rajaiah, is the new witness.

———————

20. VEDIC SCHOOL

For some of us, the pleasant evening on the banks of Kapila River at Nanjangud was a little sober. Earlier in the day, the face of the teacher with palpable helplessness, was unusual. His afternoon words was a cautious note.

"Don't fall to the curiosity to know your own 'future'. Being in the same waters, can become a brooding; even can haunt! The genuine quote from an experience in his own life signified wisdom, touching us.

When many joined the group, who are from other disciplines, it was a pleasant surprise to hear the German couple's aspirations'.

"We are looking for a new theory. It is about **'the origin of humans'**."

It is 'fascinating', but sounding serious. Many visit this place to seek an unusual, but this is intriguing. The passionate words of the German Archaeology scholar, echoed their spirits.

"It may become our pursuit in life", indicated a commitment. The ardent eyes of the couple in late thirties, cherished a mission. It is a conviction based choice.

But it appeared less linked with the 'Vedic school' at the outskirts of Mysore, a few acres of archaic set up. For centuries it is the venue to study Vedas and its appendix. After a few weeks here, the buzz of the outside world is forgotten. To share one's personal motives, like the one now, it needs some time together.

They were at ease, eager to share their views.

"We were usual students for sometimes. We believed a 'linear progress' in the human evolution. The Darwinian Theory stresses '**What the humans are**'? Our expeditions then, meant to move the concept forward."

The American John joined, "Man must have evolved 100000 years to 150000 years back."

The German continued, "The conventional theory is --- survival, adaptation to the environment; can be even the mutations; that is how what we are now, including the puzzling brain."

Now his wife joined,

"The '**Human devolution**', is the Vedic substitute to Darwinian Theory.

'A possible flow from purity to mundane'. Our existence may not be from 'the matter', but can be from the realm of 'pure consciousness'- spiritual! The humans may be combination of **matter, mind, along with spirit.**"

"Is it not a possibility that we are result of sparks of spirit, combining with the nature, to be incarnated?"

"Peter Russell even proposes a meta-paradigm for probing truth, appreciating Upanishad- 'Everything in the Universe may have, 'consciousness.' The feel which present science fails to fathom."

That was fit for listen, who are ingrained with notions of a unique culture.

His wife continued,

"When we met Michel A cremos after studying his book, 'Forbidden Archaeology", this new dimension dawned. His papers and epoch making book, "My science and my religion", induced an awe!"

"That was a turning point in us! He explained.

"One evidence to a part of Michel's theories is the discovery of human bones and artefacts in Californian gold dig, belonging to EOCENE era. Its scientifically agreed period is 50 to 55 millions of years back; it is only one of the many authentic proofs, he attests."

He concluded," Man perhaps existed, since millions of years."

Raghu immediately countered. "Why other archaeologists are ignoring it?"

"Many scientists refuse to accept it. They feel insecure to question their beliefs. We can brand it as, 'dogmas'."

"Imagine, if reluctance to tangible is so deep, how can one be open to speculative thoughts? The bigger surprise is the way science screened the 'subtle mind' or 'conscious self', by a 'Knowledge filter'.

The German couple meant serious business.

"We are fascinated by the possibility of a 'metaphysical view'! We feel some 'truths' in the otherwise labelled 'myths'?"

Finally, I quenched my thirst, "Why you are here?" "We want to study the Vedic experiments of, **'Why humans?'** instead of 'What humans?'"

"There may be a deeper reason behind 'Existence', instead of just a progressive evolvement!"

"Michel spent years to fathom the 'Vaishnavism', of the Yugas and Kalpas, for arriving to 'cyclical, cosmological' concepts. It also deals with universal, individual consciousness."

As a scientist she stressed,

"If cyclical concept were to be true, the strata of earth should reveal human existence for millions of years of periodical overlapping with artefacts and bones, which is being proved, of late".

"We are certain about the cyclical concept. But the other vital part, is the curious to explore."

The most exciting evening, ended with the words,

"We are trying to feel the essence of **'Puranic views'**, from the seers and pontiffs. One place we felt fit is the 'Brahmatantra Parakala matt' in Mysore. The next will be 'Arunadri hills' and the last at the libraries of 'Sringeri'".

It is inspiring for all. A curious depth in the quest of truth. Our reasons to be here, paled, in contrast to their sublime goals.

Nevertheless, it impacted us. Our own search based on the '**Glorious Vedas**', got a new glare.

Though the episode exemplified the **enormity of** Vedas, which is heartening emotionally, it bared a glaring distinct note.

My amusement is not for the contrast in 'belief' or 'reason'.

'Blinded affiliation, an excess in any, carries seeds of decay to swallow own tail' – Tao maxims. It begets sceptics to search 'virtue' in others'!

As usual, I am absorbed like John, with our common aim of studying one of the facets of 'Jyothishy', popularly known as' Vedic Astrology'.

Jyothishy is one of the six limbs of Vedas (The Vedangas), an integral part of the Vedic culture; an appendix of Vedas. Each appendix denotes a part of the body, like 'Jyothishy' signifying the '**eye**', with an allusion to see 'past, present and future'!

****

It was the time in the history in the end of 19th century of Mysore, when the king, "Krishna Raja Wadayar', acknowledged as the wisest was ruling the land, with a patronage to the fine arts and ancient knowledge, amidst 'prosperity' and 'leisure'.

For the mother, young wife and other pupils in the tutelage, the delicate condition of Rama Jois, is a concern. The cyclical bouts of high fever and normalcy for a few hours, is persisting for a few weeks now. It has ravaged the delicate.

The last six months were the testing times for the band of the pupils. It was when the senior Jois was summoned by the mighty King of the land of Mysore.

"My fond wish is to bring lasting peace, prosperity and happiness for the people. Consolidating the kingdom is only one aspect. My other grand aim is to preserve and pursue our heritage of knowledge and wisdom, handed over for centuries. Under Rajpurohith, the mammoth task shall begin with association of learned scholars of this holy land."

The senior Jois delegated a task under his son. To copy the original scriptures, to consolidate other data already copied and in the printed form. He focussed on touring the state, for collating all the resources on 'Jyothishy Shastra'. For the assisting pupil and Ramajois, it even became a self-learning process.

The Ayurvedic Pundit was optimistic." Am sure his soul is strong to hold on. I expect one crucial week. His weakness will increase to delirious states. Don't forget to feed the prescribed herbs tonics and liquid diet, regularly."

It was a hopeful breather, at least when the doctor was there!

––––––––––––

Rama Jois felt a drift, out from his mortal body, rising and floating. In the flight of being carried away, felt the cool breeze and the dim rays of soothing moon light. Soon he was on the imagined shringa (mountain), with the trees and the ponds, the solace of heaven. Before he could ponder whether he was alive or dead, had to close his eyes, unable to look at the beams of light descending from everywhere on to the huge platform.

When he could open his eyes, saw the unbelievable ethereal moulds, in the commune- Souls of his favourite rishis in a sharing of their thoughts.

––––––––––––

"When I arrived at the banks of Ganges under the Himalayas, I had felt that,' Am a miniature of the 'Nature' of Pancha Boothas – Air, Water, fire, Sky and Earth.' "One was recollecting.

The other added, "Yes, I had even felt the difference in each of us, by the varied degree of expressions of Nature, as Gunas in us- Tamas, Rajas and Satva."

The third felt," We wondered what propelled us to seek the road we embarked. And recollect the teacher's words."

"You are here not by chance! You will become a part of the tradition to analyse the effects of facets of Nature on humans' body and mind. It will herald a new chapter, to bring endurance and peace in mankind."

He had continued," First need is to make your mind pure and sustain it for life. Call it 'intuition' or 'instinct', but it gives insight to feel the higher modes of Nature, its finer effects. Your initial years before dipping into your own voyage is only that, apart from understanding, what I imbibed from my teachers and my experiments."

All the proud three, looked at the seer sitting at a higher pedestal, who moulded their thinking faculty, apart from their teacher.

"Mind is the only portal through which you can grasp the realities. That helps to observe, analyse. You will realise the trilogy of 'matter, mind and self'."

"Mind can only lead you to cross the bridge, to feel the consciousness, ultimately."

Rama Jois, in tears of happiness didn't observe the mist fading, the sublime scenes disappearing with the floods of sunrays. The same float which had brought him, was pushing to an unwanted return journey.

Everyone felt a new glow in his opened tired eyes.

———————

The senior Jois is back to his regular routine discussing with his pupils. He decided to expose to new levels in their experiments, with real cases of human study.

"Always note the basic difference between 'the fate' and 'the destiny'.

'Fate' is the blue print of one, when born. It reflects genetics, and karmic residues, in the form of individual build"

"One carries the effects of fate, but not limited by them. Only some effects need to be endured in the present life; 'the most' can be modified in the path of life, which is 'the destiny'. 'Destiny' is your 'freewill'. It's based on the way of life."

He then consolidated a few years of the pupils' studies.

"The modes of expressions of Nature in individuals, you have studied. They are the 'Nine Grahas'. They signify the qualities of individuals, in general. The twelve fields of each expression is the 'degree of expressions', which are 'Rashis or signs'. The static attributes in birth signifies basic natural ingredients, for body and mind.

The dynamic aspects in the flow of life is with the time dimension. The initial imprint and temporal nature's holograms in space will decide the aspects of present moments.

Now you are all ready for the practical feel. You will assist me in your new roles. The experiences will be in the 'the possible effects of nature at the moment and counter measures to contain negative possibilities'; it shall result in advices to reduce the presumed bad effects consciously.

Then you will move to your own deeper levels.

He never forgot to share his firm belief," You are not trying to reveal the clients all the possibilities. That may disturb their minds. Your focus shall be for remedies, as the Shastra suggest."

———————

Apart from the advice of withholding all the future details to clients, the other one is a curious restraint. **Senior Jois** always stressed it.

'Don't try to know your own future. You are advised to avoid it."

One pupil resisted to accept his teacher's favoured dictate..." Why sir?"

Instead of fumes in the eyes of the Guru, there was a pleading! "It is based on true experience in our ancestor's life".

At last, the shrouded oddity, specific to this tutelage, is being discussed.

"The pupil exploring any 'Vedangas', in the history of centuries, had the possibility of fascination to the 'Atherva Veda', which is associated with 'para normal'. The 'Tantric' techniques involving ritualistic practices of 'Visualisation' and 'chanting of mantras', can infuse powers of deities of nature, for the practitioner. That power has ability to be used for selfish ends, contrary to the practice of 'Jyothishy'."

"One of my grand uncles', who chanced on some scriptures appeared to have developed some mastery over some techniques, who surreptitiously practiced it. My grandfather had some clues, when his elder brother began eulogising 'visual proof' of future than by 'intuitions'."

"One day he had even remarked," Shortly will be able to see my own future, visually in the flames". But others couldn't surmise what he had seen. After a few days, my grandfather and others saw his dead body at a remote corner, in front of a still unextinguished fire inside magic geometrical figures; scores of scriptures were burnt in the fire. It was an unnatural death! That also coincided with one of his friend's absence from the tutelage."

"It is only a speculation for others. Whether he had seen anyone ending his life or retribution by nature for the half-baked powers he tried to control! Why he burnt the scriptures was startling?"

"Overall it was perhaps the excess zeal to overwhelm the nature, dissipated him."

"That day onwards such scriptures were ceremonially parted and predicting the member's own future became a taboo, here"

****

With the unusual chronicles of past stories, one dating back 115 years and the other of nearly 200 years old, there was rapt attention followed by silence in us. It had seamless transitions in renowned 'Jois' family. John, myself, Raghu and a few others' studying under a sixty plus 'Jois', are bewildered.

Jois continued." I suggest you to avoid the curiosity in your future reading, but for different reasons! Being in the same waters, possibly it can induce brooding; dissipates your energy."

It took a different turn.

"When I was born, it seems, some student predicted an unimaginable fortune for me. Even at sixty plus it haunts me. More so of late, with a wish it should happen; because if I can get it, the Ashram's continuity is assured. We are sustaining from the donations of family's Ayurvedic business now. I doubt the school's continuity in long term!"

The face of the ripened had deep worries!

We sensed his passion for the subject, and also practical helplessness. It hurt us.

John's brief tenure of six months is in the end weeks. A gems business teenager, was enthused by the therapeutic values of gems, and had an exposure to a course in the 'Vedic university' at States. His intents for finer explore to heal 'physical, mental and spiritual' situations by gems, motivated to learn under a Guru. Initially he had sensed the huge business potential. Ancient Vedic texts, 'Brihat Samhitha', and 'Garuda Purana', are brimming with the benefits of gemmology.

His big parcel from States had several gifts for colleagues and teacher. A few months had clearly softened him, rendering humanistic.

"More than the knowledge I gained, it is the company of friends and affection showed, I am carrying. I had never imagined such a possibility, which is so beautiful. I will cherish it for lifetime!"

Inexplicably, after presenting me with a golden ring with a Jade, was all the praise for it. "Jade is for serenity, and harmony for the life, a soothing charm of light for stability."

He is extolling its virtues. "The Neptune's subtlety, can advance human consciousness to higher levels"

He even shared the commercial aspects.

"Pure Jade referred to, 'Jadeite', depending on rarity, quality, carat value and its deeper colour can cost millions. The original stones found very rarely, including imperial ones, are fancied acquisitions in the world."

"Even the semiprecious 'Jades' are curative, costing a few tens of dollars to hundreds. For the Buddhists and Hindus with religious inclines, idols of 'Buddha' or 'Ganesh' in jade, are worthy possessions, more valued than gold."

When parting from the place which has influenced him to be to a better human and knowledgeable, he was emotional. He prostrated to the feet of the teacher, 'Jois', with a tearful note of gratitude. Standing before the elevated altar, which had a statue of 'Sharadha devi', the goddess of learning and wisdom, closed his eyes and prayed with longer meditative stance. His last respects was also to the semi- precious stones and 'the Saligramas' of Nepal and Himalayas accumulated over centuries, decorated on the base pedestal of the huge statue.

Before I concluded my own course on the 'Vaastu', an incredible joy for the teacher was heartening. One of his students in anonymity from abroad, had presented him a fortune of a couple of millions of dollars. With a history of tens of students from abroad in the decades, he was unable to isolate the identity.

On the next auspicious day of the Dasara festive, the cleaning of the idol and the altar was my usual ritual, once in a year.

When I was cleaning the 'Jade', supposed to be one of the gifts from 'Vijaynagar emperor' hundreds of years back, remembered John.

But more curious was the jade looking definitely different compared to last year.

> The Jade was perceptibly 'less heavy, of lighter tint and less attractive!'

_____

About the Author

Born in Mysore, a culture city near Bangalore, graduated in science and later, in Engineering with Electronics subject. For three decades associated with design Labs of the country, in path-breaking missiles, Light Combat Aircraft designs. Head of a Design lab, advisor to a German firm, had tenures at USA, UK and USSR, of diverse cultures. Is training poor bright from his town, for engineering entrance.

Printed in the United States
By Bookmasters